The Witch of Halloween House

Jeff DeGordick

Copyright © 2017 by Jeff DeGordick

All rights reserved. No part of this publication may be reproduced or transmitted in any form or by any means, electronic, mechanical or otherwise, without written permission from the author.

This is a work of fiction. Names, characters, businesses, places, events and incidents are either the products of the author's imagination or used in a fictitious manner. Any resemblance to actual persons, living or dead, or actual events is purely coincidental.

Cover images copyright © Shutterstock

Visit my website for FREE stories and news of future releases, promotions, and sales:
www.jeffdegordick.com

Say hello on my Facebook and Twitter page:
www.facebook.com/jeffdegordickauthor
www.twitter.com/jeffdegordick

I'm happy to hear from my readers! Send me an email at:
jeff@jeffdegordick.com

Also by Jeff DeGordick:
The Haunting of Bloodmoon House
The Haunting of Jingle House

— CHAPTER ONE —

BLAZE

By the time the police chief arrived on the scene, word of the child's disappearance spread like wildfire through the town, creating a panic.

Chief Robert Miller pulled the cruiser to a stop in the parking lot at the edge of the woods and opened the door. Stepping out into the crisp October air, he squinted his eyes at the wind, peering through the night. He already saw his deputy up ahead standing at the edge of the woods next to Lorraine Basham.

Don gave him a concerned glance. "It doesn't look good, Boss," he said. His words were barely audible as Mrs. Basham started up on Robert as he approached.

She threw herself into his arms, bleating against him like a miserable and dying goat. "My son!" she cried. "My son!"

Robert held her at arm's length and regarded her carefully. "What happened, Mrs. Basham?" His voice was calm and smooth as stone; it was something he had built up in the face of pressure after years on the job.

"My David!" Mrs. Basham wailed. "He's gone!" She waved her arms around them, and Robert followed her gestures, trying to put the pieces together where her words couldn't. "I-I-I went to the store to get some butter," she said, pointing at the small mart by the parking lot. "I just went in to get some butter, and when I came out he was gone!" She spun around in a circle, gazing out at the woods, as if searching its perimeter for the thirtieth time would make him reappear.

Robert planted his hands firmly on her shoulders and looked her square in the eye. "Was there anyone else around? Did you see anyone?"

She shook her head in tears.

"Boss, there's something else you gotta see," his deputy said. There was an uneasiness in his eyes that revealed bad news. Robert knew that one, too.

He followed Don to the start of the woods as Mrs. Basham clung to them like a shadow, tightly kneading her hands together. When he stopped suddenly and turned, Robert looked down and saw exactly what he meant to show him.

There was a small shoe that looked to be the right size for a young boy, and sitting next to it, a few feet away, was a half-eaten gingerbread man. Robert bent down.

"Mrs. Basham said he got the cookie from home," Don commented. His eyes flicked over to the shoe, telling Robert that that was the pertinent piece of evidence.

Robert glanced over at it and pulled a plastic glove out, sliding it over his hand. He carefully picked up the shoe and turned it over, shining a flashlight on it. Around one side of the shoe that he hadn't seen so far, as well as the sole, a thin layer of sticky red blood coated it.

"Ah jeez," Robert said, immediately feeling the rest of his words hike up in his throat. He wished he hadn't said it; he always kept himself composed in front of relatives of victims, but this was a sight that he never got used to.

The first specks of rain came from the cloudy night sky overhead and fell on his arm. Robert glanced up at it, then he looked over at his deputy. "Bag this up quickly. Then get the rest of the guys here, pronto. I want this area scoured before the rain comes in."

Don nodded. "You got it, Boss." He set off.

"I'll get a search party," Robert added, and Don nodded again. He stood up and faced Mrs. Basham, who was still just as beside herself as when he arrived. Consoling people was the other part of the job that he never got used to.

As the night went on, the rain broke out fully and came down hard. The search teams were organized and sweeping the woods with flashlights and police dogs. Any other complements that the local townspeople could help out with was more than welcomed. It was a small town, and everybody knew each other. The best perk of that was that everybody helped each other, too, and had a strong community mindset. But no matter how much they searched the woods, tearing it inside and out from one end to the other, they just couldn't find the boy, and their hearts collectively sank.

But there was one outlier to their community. A single house sat atop a hill deep in those woods. There were no roads going to it, and nobody ever went close, save for the old woman who lived there.

She rarely was spotted in public, mostly living as a recluse. She never interacted with anyone, and her mysterious nature caused rumors to spread over the years. Most of the kids thought she was an honest to goodness witch; the adults were merely wary of her.

But now that little David had been missing and became a public concern, eyes and attention quickly turned to the lonely house on the hill and the frail and secretive woman who occupied it.

Their search parties turned up nothing, and the townsfolk quickly demanded that Robert search the house. He was reluctant at first, wanting to leave things like that well enough alone if he could, but he got a warrant and went up the next night—two nights before Halloween—and served it on her.

He rapped on the door loudly.

"Think she'll answer?" Don asked.

Robert made a sound as if to laughingly dismiss such an absurd idea. He knocked again.

They could both hear her shuffling inside, and even the woman's footsteps weren't normal; they had a strange, uneven rhythm that seemed more like an animal dragging its claws across the floor.

"Ma'am, we have a search warrant!" Robert announced. He banged on the door with his fist. When he didn't get an answer, he turned to Don and rolled his eyes, grabbing the doorknob.

Don tensed up, his hand gliding across his hip to his gun.

Robert jiggled the handle, but it wouldn't open.

More shuffling inside.

The darkness bore down on them from all around. It wasn't raining, but it was ice cold. The chill imparted a strong uneasiness that both of them felt, though Robert did a better job of hiding it. They were apprehensive enough standing before such a strange looking house; it was modest in size, but peculiar in appearance. Everything about its construction just looked off, like someone took the blueprints to a normal home and skewed it every fourth step. The roof was lopsided, some of the shingles drooped over the edge, the framing of the door and windows were slanted.

"Ma'am, were coming in!" Robert said in a booming voice. He took a step back then kicked in the door. The flimsy wood didn't stand a chance against the force and it slammed into the wall inside, emitting a loud crack throughout the interior.

Robert stepped in first and then Don. The inside of the house was just as peculiar as the outside, and it seemed to be the abode of a hoarder. Seemingly ancient pieces of furniture peeked out from underneath a mountain of garbage and junk. Strange trinkets littered the tiny room they were in, either hanging off crooked nails in the wall, sitting on crooked shelves, or strewn across the rest of the junk.

A strong odor overwhelmed them, more pungent than anything they'd ever smelled. It was something akin to rotten onions or cabbage, but there was an exotic accent to it as well.

A dingy light bulb loosely hanging from the ceiling cast the room in a sickly yellow glow. Robert glanced up at it and saw a moth flutter, gently battering itself against the glass. A cold draft blew through a doorway in front of them, and Don went on ahead, glancing over his shoulder at his chief. He apprehensively took another step for the darkness beyond. His heart rate quickened.

The bizarre footsteps started up again from the blackness, rushing for him. He took a step back, and his hand tightened around his pistol.

Wails echoed, loud and unintelligible, and the woman stormed into the room.

Robert and Don backed up, both of their bodies tensing up, but not acting on their fright.

The old woman was hunched over terribly at the waist with a large hump for a back. Tattered black rags hung over her deformed body like a dusty, spider-infested tablecloth in a haunted house. An odd black hat hung off the back of her head. Whatever shape it had originally been was indiscernible, because it had apparently been flattened and warped over the years. The only parts of her skin that were visible were her hands and her face. Her skin was old and tanned, filled with bumps and strange abrasions. Stringy white hair came out from under the hat and fell over top of the robes, damply clinging to the sides of her face. Her nose was long and crooked, and her eyes were sunk deep into her skull, yet they were wide and bulging. The whites of them seemed to have turned yellow, and Robert couldn't tell if she had a medical condition, or if it was just the effect of the old light bulb.

The woman raised her hands in the air, but with her poor posture, they didn't go any higher than her shoulders. She took a few shuffling steps toward Robert, her tiny chin falling open as her toothless mouth hurled a series of objections that were somewhere between incomprehensible mutters and an exotic tongue.

Robert took another step back, easing his hand off his gun. He held a hand up to her. "Ma'am. Ma'am!" he said forcefully, trying to cut through her cries. "We have a warrant to search your house!" He pulled it out and showed it to her. Her bulging eyes glanced at it for only a moment before she swiped it away and it fell to the floor. Don kept a keen eye on her as Robert calmly picked it up. "Ma'am, a young boy went missing in the woods near your house last night," he explained. "We need to search the premises to make sure he's not here."

The old woman's nattering didn't skip a beat.

"Ma'am, have you seen anyone in the woods around your house?" Don tried. But the woman didn't even look at him, much less understand him.

The two men gave a defeated look to each other, shrugging and pushing forward.

Robert shouldered his way past the unhelpful woman as he turned on a flashlight and moved deeper into the small home. He relied on Don to watch his back, knowing that the deputy would be overwhelmingly paranoid anyway at the odd situation.

They swept through the house, finding a set of stairs that went down to an even smaller basement. Everything was grimy and littered, and the basement was no exception. Robert's feet sank down into spongy floorboards when he got to the bottom of the stairs, and he thought how strange it was to have a wooden floor in a basement. The entire house was off in nearly every conceivable way, like the woman had hammered it together herself with mismatched scraps.

Robert wore gloves as he dug through some of the junk, much to the continued protests of the woman. But after a while she settled down, eventually even falling silent and letting the two police officers carry out their search warrant. But as much as they dug and sifted through dirty piles, they came up with nothing. Furthermore, despite how funny the woman and her house were, neither officer even had the intuition that the boy was here.

Regretfully, they apologized for disturbing the woman and left the house. When they stepped back out into the dark and cold woods, a voice carried through the trees.

"Is he there?"

Robert turned his head and saw Jim Falwell, a regular at the local bar. "What are you doing here, Jim?" Robert asked.

"Well?" Jim asked, ignoring him. "Is he there?" Tears welled up in his eyes. "What did she do to him?"

Robert's gaze fell on the hammer Jim clutched in his hand and was subtly hiding behind his leg. His eyes turned up to the man's face, silently telling him what he thought about doing something so stupid.

Jim's stare fell.

"Get out of here," Robert warned. "I don't want to see you back up here, you understand?" He rubbed a hand across his mustache and felt the stubble growing in on his chin. He knew he would have to make a statement to the townspeople soon to calm them down. The last thing he wanted was a witch hunt on his hands.

But a statement late that night did no good. The townspeople were upset and angry. Their search parties turned up nothing, they still had no answers about what happened to little David Basham, and they feared the worst. The rumors circulated more viciously and tempers and paranoia flared, despite Robert's efforts to quell them.

On Halloween night, a large mob of the townspeople marched up to the old woman's house in the woods, surrounding it and demanding justice. A respectful but now tenuous relationship between the townspeople and their chief of police kept them from outright barging in and killing the woman. Members of the crowd cycled in and out throughout the evening. Gary Dunburger, a retired woodworker, didn't have a torch to bring, so he brought a jack-o'-lantern he'd carved instead. The idea caught on, and soon all who came to the house marched up the wooded hill with their lit pumpkins. They placed them all around the house, a surrounding army of leering and demented orange faces staring at the woman.

The people sometimes shouted things, sometimes picked up small rocks and chucked them at the dilapidated exterior. Robert sent a few of his men to warn the crowd away, but they wouldn't listen, and he didn't want to strain their relationship to the breaking point.

Robert sat at his desk in the station just before 9pm. He leaned forward on his elbows and rubbed his fingers into his temples, trying to get the strain out of them.

His kids were at home while he was stuck at the station. He'd charged his teenage daughter with taking her little brother out to go trick-or-treating, and an errant thought ran through his mind, wondering how he would react if it were his own son that had been taken.

Just as he shook off the chill that coursed through his body like an icy wave, Don rounded the corner and just about slid into his office.

"Bob, we found him!" he said.

Robert lifted his head off his hands. "What?"

"We found David!" Don said. "He turned up!"

"Where?"

"He came back home! He said a coyote attacked him and he ran away into the woods and got lost... almost ended up in the next county over. But he found his way back! Lorraine just called."

THE WITCH OF HALLOWEEN HOUSE

The relief that washed over Robert only lasted for a second before the squawk of the radio sitting on his desk shattered it into pieces.

He picked it up. "Say again?"

"The mob set the old woman's house on fire!" one of his men shouted over the other end.

"No..." Robert muttered. His hand felt like ice and it slowly sank onto the desk as the radio tumbled out of it.

--- --- ---

The blaze lit up the dark sky like a giant bonfire. Hot orange flames licked dangerously close to the nearby trees, and if they didn't find a way to put it out, the whole forest might have been at risk.

But all Robert could do was stand there helplessly and watch as the fire raged, consuming the entire ground floor of the demented house.

A terrible scream erupted from inside. It intensified both in volume and in anguish. Eventually, the screams were snuffed out as the flames engulfed everything.

The fire department had been called, but with no roads leading up to the house, there was nothing they could do. They called the state and told them that they'd keep them updated, but they knew by the time they got a chopper over to dump chemicals on the blaze, it would already have burned out.

Most of the mob that surrounded the house had dispersed, but a small group remained. Robert looked each one of them in the eye, and he could see the fear and regret in each one of them.

Damn you, he thought. *Damn you*.

A spittle of rain fell on them, and before long, the clouds bunched up and dumped a strong rainfall on the area. The fire still raged for many hours into the night, and it wasn't until a couple hours before dawn that the last embers were extinguished.

The firefighters came up the hill on foot, as did the paramedics. As the firefighters came out of the blackened shell of the house, they yelled to the medics that there was a body inside. They went in with a narrow backboard and emerged a few minutes later with the charred body of the old woman strapped to it. She was so short and uneven that she only took up half of it, tipped over to one side. Her charred face pointed at Robert as the medics walked by with her. Then she unexpectedly writhed and moaned, causing one of the paramedics to falter and have to get his footing. They stopped in front of Robert and he stared down at the woman with wide, terrified eyes.

Her own eyes opened. What little life was left in her would soon be gone, but she was still conscious. Her eyes swam in her head before falling on Robert's face. Then they narrowed with a look of hatred. She wiggled her arm out of the restraints and extended a long and bony finger toward his face.

"A curse," the woman said. "A curse on all of you!"

The medics looked down at her, stunned.

Then the woman shrieked and twisted violently on the board. And before any of them could decide what to do, the woman turned to ash before their very eyes.

The paramedics dropped the backboard in fear, and the dust of the woman sifted through the air.

As Robert stared down at the woman's remains, a terror gripped his heart. He shifted his gaze out to the town below as a cold and brooding wind picked up.

— CHAPTER TWO —

Night Flight

Three years later, Robert passed the peas.

"Thanks," his daughter Carmen said, grabbing the bowl and spooning a heaping pile onto her plate. She extended it out to her brother Tommy, but he just shook his head with a sour look on his face.

The family ate in silence for a long time before Robert broke it. "So what are you kids going to do tonight when I'm at work?" he asked.

Carmen and Tommy looked at each other, shrugging.

"I don't know, maybe watch a movie or something?" Carmen suggested. "As long as he doesn't act like a little brat, that is." She rustled his hair and he shrunk away from her. He always hated it when his big sister did that. But she was only joking; her brother was one of the most well-adjusted and best kids around.

"You *better* keep him in line," Robert said with a chuckle. "You're the big woman of the family now." He added the second part in good spirits, but as soon as he'd said it, his face fell. All of theirs did. He looked down at the wedding band on his finger and fiddled with it. It felt heavier these days, like a shackle. He didn't know exactly why he still wore it... maybe just to give the kids a semblance of normalcy, or maybe to remind them that they were still the same family they were when their mom was still around. But he missed her terribly, so he tried to chew the tension away in his jaw with the roast beef in his mouth.

"Dad..." Tommy said rather timidly, "...can you, um... take me trick-or-treating this year?" He regarded his dad with wide and fearful eyes, like he was afraid of what he was going to say.

Robert swallowed the mashed potatoes in his mouth, then wiped his lips. "We'll see," he said. He saw his son's face fall in disappointment, and he hated that look. "You know how busy I am. Things are quiet right now, so I'll try my best, but you know how the job is."

Tommy sullenly nodded.

"Hey, it's not so bad," he added, trying to lighten the mood. "If I can't make it, your sister can always take you."

"She always takes me," he complained. "She's taken me every year since Mom..." His face turned away.

Robert's heart strained. He hated seeing his children like this. It was always his wife that was the grand matriarch of the family, the nurturer who took care of all the odds and ends while he worked hard to provide a good life for all of them. But after she passed away three and a half years ago, all of the burdens of life fell on him. And sometimes it was difficult to shoulder.

Carmen took up the slack as much as she could. Losing her mother had been terrible, but she pulled through it as best as she could for her little brother's sake. She was ten years his senior and just a year into college now, and she did everything she could to help out her family and put a smile on their faces.

She nudged her brother in the shoulder. "Cheer up, I'm not so bad, am I?"

Tommy just turned and stuck his tongue out at her.

"Hey!" Carmen cried. She flicked him on the arm, and Tommy retaliated by loading up a pea on his spoon and launching it at her.

A minor food fight ensued, but Robert held a hand up and quashed it quickly. "Okay, okay, you two."

They all settled down and finished up their dinner. At a quarter to seven when he was ready for his shift, Robert said goodbye to his kids.

"Make sure he doesn't get into trouble," he said to Carmen in confidence.

"I will," she replied, standing next to him by the door. "I love you, Daddy." She stretched up on her toes and kissed him on the cheek.

He reached out and wrapped his large hand around hers and squeezed. "Love you too, Sweetpea." And with a smile, he opened the door and left for his shift.

Carmen watched the darkness swallow him as he headed for his cruiser. She shut the door and thought about taking Tommy trick-or-treating.

Everything had quickly gone back to normal after the horrific incident three years prior. The townspeople had been so ashamed by what they'd done that nobody talked about it at all anymore. Robert never figured out exactly who set the fire, but at this point it didn't matter. What happened was, and forever would be, a dark stain on their small town.

Carmen remembered it vividly from an outside view. She and her brother only got secondhand details from their father when he wasn't busy, and taking Tommy trick-or-treating that year was like walking through a ghost town. Half the town was too upset to even put out candy or take their own kids trick-or-treating, and the other half had stormed up the hill, demanding justice from the woman they mistakenly thought kidnapped David. The last two years had been normal, but each time, the frightening thought of her brother going missing or being kidnapped filled her thoughts.

She walked to the end of the hall and gently pushed open her brother's door. It seemed like the room was empty at first, and her heart lurched.

"Tommy?"

"...What?"

"Where are you?" she asked, searching around the room. Then she noticed the sheets on his bed were strewn haphazardly across it, with one side seemingly extending out into the air. She walked around the bed and saw that he had made himself a little cubby under the blanket in the narrow gap between his bed and the wall.

Tommy was lying on his stomach in the makeshift cubbyhole, reading an old Hardy Boys book by flashlight.

"*The Ghost at Skeleton Rock*..." Carmen read off the cover. "What's that, like your thirtieth Hardy Boys book?"

His eyes shifted up in thought. "No, only twenty-two." He turned his attention back to the book. "It's so cool! They found a clue in this ventriloquist's dummy, and now there's this tropical island they have to go to."

Carmen smiled. Her little brother loved adventure books, and in many ways he was still (and she hoped he always would be) curious and innocently mischievous. Even after their mother passed away, he kept his upbeat spirit, and that had helped her through a lot of hard times.

"I heard there's treasure buried at the school, you know," he said suddenly.

"At the school?"

"Yeah, buried in the playground."

"And who told you that?" Carmen asked, already feeling like she knew the answer.

"Brett did," Tommy replied. "Him, Randy and Shawn are going to go there tonight at eight. I want to go with them and find it!"

Carmen gave him a stern look. "You're not going anywhere, mister."

His face twisted into a mixture of shock and disappointment. He was a good kid, but he didn't take kindly to being told no. "Aw, come on, *please?* Dad doesn't have to know!"

"Do you know what dad will do to us—do to *me*—if he finds that you snuck out while he was gone? Tommy, he showed me the bullet."

Tommy didn't want to be deterred, but he knew he didn't have a leg to stand on.

Carmen turned around and sat on the floor, awkwardly leaning against the bed just under the sheet extending over them. "Besides, I don't want you hanging around Brett, anyway."

"I know you think he's a '*bad apple*'," Tommy said.

"No, his two little lackeys are bad apples. He's a *rotten* apple."

"All bad apples are rotten apples," Tommy said.

"Whatever. You know what I mean. He's nothing but a troublemaker and a delinquent. Him and his sister, too."

"A delinq... what?" Tommy said.

"Never mind," Carmen replied. "Just enjoy your book." She turned to him and sternly put a finger in his face. "Remember, no sneaking out. A living family is a happy family."

Tommy set the book down. "Fine," he said sheepishly. "So, are you going to take me for a costume?"

"What do you mean?" Carmen asked.

"For Halloween," he said. "It's only in three days."

"Oh, right." She went through the calendar in her head and couldn't believe how fast time flew. "I'll take you to the store tomorrow and get you something. What do you want to go as?"

"Joe Hardy!" he cried.

"Hmm, so like a red sweater? That would be a pretty lame costume."

"You're lame!"

Carmen kicked at the bed sheet attached to the wall, pulling the tape away and making it fall on him.

"Hey!" he shouted, re-taping it to the wall.

Carmen turned and left the room, giggling. She went to the living room and plunked on the couch. She turned on the TV and mindlessly flipped through the channels for a while, tired after a long day of school. She ran through a list of things to do that night in her head and tried to prioritize them, but she soon realized that she didn't want to do a single thing. Finally, she admitted defeat and got up. She decided that she needed to take a shower, so she walked back to Tommy's room to let him know.

When she pushed the door open again, she didn't see him anywhere. "You're *still* reading?" she asked. She walked around his bed and bent down to look in the cubby, but he wasn't there. "Tommy?" She pressed herself down to her stomach and looked under the bed, then she stood up and looked in his closet, but he wasn't anywhere. She spun around, about to go down the hallway, when she felt a cold breeze wash over the back of her neck.

Her heart pounding, she turned around.

The window to his bedroom was wide open and his curtains fluttered in the night breeze.

Tommy was gone.

— CHAPTER THREE —

GINGERBREAD

Carmen blew hot air into her hands to warm them up as she rushed down the street. She only had enough time to hastily throw on a coat on her way out the door, and now the cold wind nipped at her cheeks, giving them a rosy hue.

She silently seethed under her breath, trying to decide how she was going to kill her little brother when she found him. At least she knew where he went.

The school was several blocks away from their house, and the only car they had at home was her father's police cruiser, so she was used to walking and taking the bus around town. It would take her a while to get there, and she tried to figure out what path Tommy would have taken to see if she could catch him on the way.

She didn't at all trust Brett or his ilk. They were in the same school grade as Tommy, and she didn't think that anyone could find a more reprobated bunch if they tried. She'd heard many first-hand stories about Brett from her father, though thankfully she never had much interaction with him herself. Robert told her of a time where he deliberately started a fire in the school's kitchen, and about another time when he had snuck into the vehicle pool in the back of the police station, trying to break into a cruiser, as well as a host of other incidents. Carmen didn't know what he had in mind for her brother, but she knew it certainly had nothing to do with "treasure".

Carmen reached the main street of the town heading into their tiny downtown area, if they could call it that. A few cars rolled by, and some people were still out walking along from store to store, though the crowds were dwindling at this hour.

She rounded the corner and cut onto Rosedale Avenue, and a funny feeling hit her. She stumbled, using the brick wall of the store next to her to prop herself up. Her head felt strange, like she was dizzy and about to pass out. She waited for the moment to pass, wondering if she hadn't had enough to eat or if something was disagreeing with her, but it didn't end. She squeezed her eyes shut and leaned fully against the wall, pressing her palms to her temples. The feeling was indescribable, almost like a worm digging through her brain.

And then in the next moment, it was gone.

Carmen stood upright and blinked her eyes a few times. She had never experienced anything like that before, and it frightened her. She momentarily forgot about her brother as she tried to figure out what happened to her, then she was struck by another feeling: anger.

She was confused. This feeling was completely familiar to her, but she couldn't figure out why on earth she was feeling it now. There was no reason she should have been angry about anything. She was upset with her brother, sure, but she was more frightened for his safety and the trouble he was getting in, than angry.

As she started to move down the street again, shrugging off the odd experience, she spotted the Wilsons in a parked car across the street. They were an older couple in their seventies, and as she peered at them through the window, it seemed like Mr. Wilson had a look of anguish on his face. His wife was twisted around in her seat, caring for him, and then he began to make gestures as if he was telling her that he was okay. A moment later, the car lurched forward and they rolled off out of view.

Carmen paused again, watching the car go.

The streets emptied out a bit, and all she heard was the soft hooting of an owl in a nearby tree. She spotted it sitting atop a high branch. The owl's head was cocked toward her and its wide eyes stared. Carmen glanced away as she walked, but then when she looked back, she saw that the owl was still gazing at her. Feeling frightened now, she watched its head track her movement with every step she took.

She swallowed hard and picked up the pace.

― ― ―

The school was quiet and the whole place was empty, except for one last late worker.

The four boys huddled behind a row of bushes at the perimeter of the property, watching as the front door of the school opened. Mr. Pabodie strode out, turning and locking the doors, before heading off to the last car in the parking lot.

"There he goes," Brett said, watching him.

"About time," Randy said excitedly. He bounced up and down on his knees a little from behind the bush, like he was ready to take off sprinting or he had to go to the bathroom.

Tommy crouched down next to them, feeling the cold bite of the wind on the back of his neck. He looked off toward the playground at the side of the schoolyard. They would have to wait for Mr. Pabodie to leave so he didn't spot them, but then it looked like they had the run of the place. "So it's buried under the slide?" he asked.

"Yeah, totally," Brett said slyly.

"And he's off," Randy announced, still bouncing.

The car backed up away from the parking stop, then it pulled forward and drove out of the lot onto Winegrass Road.

"Let's go!" Brett said. He tagged Randy and Shawn on the shoulder, then he cast a glance down at Tommy as he stood. "Well, you comin'?"

Tommy hesitated a moment, then he nodded his head. He really wanted to find the treasure that Brett told him was buried there, but something felt off about everything. Maybe it was the darkness or the cold, or the spookiness that saturated the couple weeks leading up to Halloween, but he was uncomfortable. Regardless, he got to his feet and followed the three kids.

They skirted along the edge of the parking lot to the playground, and Brett walked past the jungle gym to the row of swings at the back. There was a set of four, and three of them took a seat with Tommy lagging behind.

"I thought you said it was under the slide," Tommy said.

"Nah, I've got it right here," Brett replied coolly. He reached into his jacket and pulled out a pack of cigarettes. Randy's eyes lit up as he fidgeted on the swing, and Shawn just stared at Brett quietly.

"Where'd you get that?" Tommy choked out.

"My sister's boyfriend," Brett replied. He slid a cigarette halfway out the pack. "You ever try one?"

"N-no."

Brett held the pack out to him, and Tommy could quickly see the smile on his face fading the more he hesitated.

"Well? Take it! You want to hang out with us, don't you?"

Tommy didn't say anything, but he reached out and took the cigarette, holding it up in his fingers and feeling the texture and shape of the strange object. Brett passed the pack around to Randy and Shawn, who each took one.

"Who's got the lighter?" Brett asked.

"Right here." Shawn produced a BIC lighter.

Brett took it and flicked the wheel, holding the flame out to Tommy. There was a look of glee dancing across his face, and for a second, Tommy thought he saw the face of the devil himself flash across it.

He carefully slid the end of the cigarette between his lips and leaned his neck out for the lighter. He didn't really know what was going on, but he wanted to fit in.

A sharp pain tore at his ear, and Tommy yelled in agony. He was yanked off the swing and dragged up to his feet until he was stretched on his toes to accommodate the harsh tug.

The other boys' heads twisted around and saw Carmen holding her little brother by the ear, a nasty scowl on her face.

"Just what do you think you're doing?" she demanded of her brother.

He opened his mouth to speak and the cigarette tumbled to the ground. "I... I..."

Carmen gave him a yank and let him stumble away from the group, then she turned her attention to the three boys sitting on the swing set who looked like deer caught in the headlights. "And you three," she seethed. She turned her ire on Brett specifically, marching up to him and grabbing him by the ear, too.

"Hey!" he protested. He always tried to act cool and tough, but he didn't stand much of a chance in front of a nineteen-year-old, even if she was a girl.

"You guys are nine, for God's sake!" Carmen shouted. She ripped the pack out of his hand and threw it on the ground, stomping on it.

"Let go of him!" a voice shrieked from the darkness.

Carmen spun around and saw the miserable Stacy Stalworth, Brett's sister. When Brett saw her, he smirked, then he shoved himself away from Carmen and broke free of her grip.

Stacy wore about two pounds of makeup and big hoop earrings, and she marched right up into Carmen's face. She gave Carmen a little shove, but Carmen stood her ground. "What the hell are you doing grabbing my brother?!" she demanded.

"Don't give me that," Carmen started. "I'm not going to let your lying, little scamp of a brother corrupt mine."

Brett stood emboldened behind the protection of his sister. Tommy stood to Carmen's side, staring at the ground in shame. The other two boys were just bystanders caught in the crossfire, looking bewildered at the fight.

Stacy stuck a manicured fingernail in front of Carmen's face, curving it like a talon. "You touch him again, and no boy's ever gonna want to look at your face again." She scoffed. "Not that you get any attention now, anyway." She pulled a wad of gum out of her mouth and flicked it at Carmen. It bounced off her cheek and caught momentarily on her shoulder before falling to the grass.

Carmen scowled, but she chose not to rise to the challenge. She stood nose to nose with Stacy and glared into her eyes.

"Come on, Brett," Stacy said, grabbing him by the arm and dragging him away. There was a car sitting at the end of the parking lot with the window rolled down, and a man that looked to be in his late twenties, older than all of them, sat in the driver's seat, a baseball cap on his head and a messy goatee covering his chin.

Brett turned around as she dragged him and shot Carmen a triumphant look. "Later, you dweeb," he said to Tommy.

Randy and Shawn retreated to the car, but after the young man inside looked at them and shook his head, they quietly stumbled off down the street by themselves.

Carmen turned to Tommy who was still staring at his shoes. "You have got a lot of explaining to do, mister."

"I... I didn't know," he said.

"Didn't know what?" she started.

A scream blared into the night from somewhere nearby.

Both of them spun around and looked in the direction it came from.

Another scream followed, trailed by a long, wailing moan.

The hairs stood up on the backs of their necks.

"What was that?" Tommy asked.

"I don't know," Carmen replied. The screams put her on edge. There was such terror and anguish in them, that whatever situation caused them had to be downright unthinkable.

Tommy started off by himself.

"Hey, where are you going?!" Carmen asked, catching up to him.

"I want to see what that was."

"No," Carmen said, "we should get home. It's not safe out here." She looked around at the shadows engulfing them, thinking about her strange experience before and wondering if something malicious was lurking around.

"What if someone's in trouble?" he asked.

Another wail filled the air, this one less terrorized and more just full of pain. It was coming from a residential stretch at the edge of the downtown area.

Carmen hesitated, but when she looked and saw her brother's eyes, they convinced her. They were wide and concerned, full of her brother's good nature and sense of justice. "Fine," she said. "But you've been reading too many Hardy Boys books."

The two of them set off as the person moaned into the night.

"I think it's Mrs. Darton," Tommy said as they ran.

Carmen thought he was right. The voice sounded similar, but she couldn't possibly imagine what tragedy had befallen her. She lived in a house on a big piece of property that stretched out into the woods in the back.

When they got to her house, they pinpointed her voice to her backyard. Mrs. Darton stood next to a dip in the ground that cut across the yard on an angle, with the woods on the other side. There were already two locals standing next to her and consoling her, with another one venturing into the woods.

"What's going on?" Carmen asked.

Mrs. Darton's face was beet-red, a wet mess of tears. "My-my son!" she choked out. "He's missing!" She buried her face into the chest of another resident and continued sobbing.

Carmen and Tommy stood rigid like boards. Their gazes drifted over to the child-sized shoe that she was clutching, and suddenly their minds went back three years to little David Basham. Then when they saw the gingerbread cookie sitting at her feet, their blood turned to ice.

Carmen unconsciously wrapped her arm around Tommy and squeezed him tightly to herself.

— CHAPTER FOUR —

THE CARVING IN THE TREE

Robert sat at his desk at the station, his head cradled in his hands. The phone rang. He picked it up and answered. Nodding along as the information came through the line, he pulled a pad of paper and a pen across the desk to him and took down the information. Thanking the person for the tip, he put the phone back on the cradle, dropped the pen, and returned his head to his hands.

Various tips had been coming in all night, most of them unhelpful. No one had seen anything, and even the mother didn't know anything about her son's disappearance, other than the fact that he had been playing in the backyard. Most people who called just wanted to know what was happening.

Robert already organized search parties and was coordinating and relaying information between them. Word of the disappearance spread very quickly, just like last time, only this time the townspeople didn't have a boogeyman to blame. But the whole thing was strange and frightening. He went through every detail, trying to make sense of it.

His mind went back to the old woman who burned to death in her house. The image he'd seen of her painfully twisting and turning into ash was burned into his memory. The bizarre event haunted him to this day. "*A curse... A curse on all of you!*" she had said.

Could it have been her? he thought. *Could it* still *be her?* A moment later, the thought drifted out of his head. It was too absurd. But the details were very striking: the boy had disappeared in the woods just like David Basham three years ago; a lone shoe had been found in his place, though no blood on it this time; and a gingerbread cookie had been found at the scene, although in this case it hadn't been eaten at all. *A copycat?* he thought.

This was the last thing the town needed, especially on Halloween.

The phone rang again, and he reluctantly answered it. When the call finished, he placed the phone on the cradle and started to draw his hand away, but then he paused. He stared at the phone, hesitated for another moment, then he plucked it up again and dialed his house.

Carmen picked up on the third ring. "Hello?"

"It's me, Sweetpea."

"Dad! What's going on? Did you find him?"

Robert wiped his hand across his tired face. "No, not yet." His eyes drifted up the blank wall in front of him. "I just wanted to see how you two are doing."

"We're okay... it's just kind of scary, you know?"

Robert silently nodded with the phone pressed to his ear. "Yeah honey, I know. Just keep your brother inside this time, okay?"

"Yeah, I will, Dad."

"You promise?" There was fear in his voice.

Carmen sensed this, and her answer was slow and hesitant. "Yeah... yeah, Dad, I will. Promise."

Robert said goodbye and hung up the phone, then leaned back in his chair. He shuffled around the photos they'd taken at the scene on his desk as the gears turned in his head. The phone rang again.

— — —

Carmen stared out the window in the living room, looking over their darkened front lawn and into the neighborhood beyond. It had been two minutes since she'd seen a car roll by, and now with each passing second, an evil and mysterious force closed in around the house; she could feel it. And every time she took a deep breath, it was pushed back a little. Her heart thumped. Everything around outside was still. Even the breeze had abated completely, and she waited for something to happen as her eyes flicked from one dark corner to another.

Something jabbed her in the back. "Hey."

Carmen jumped and spun around.

"Sorry," Tommy said fearfully. "What are you doing?"

Carmen settled down. "Nothing," she said.

He walked past her to the window and looked out, seeing the same still and yet terrifying sights that she had. "Are you going to take me trick-or-treating?"

Carmen laughed. "Really? You're asking me this now?"

"I want to go this year," he mumbled. "I hate it when this happens."

"Tommy, I don't think it's such a good idea this year. We don't even know what's going on yet."

"But—"

"It's not safe," she added.

He didn't say anything. He had both of his palms pressed flat to the glass and leaned his forehead against the cold surface. He opened his mouth and breathed out hot air, fogging it up. Then he took his forefinger and traced a shape in the condensation.

"What are you doing?" Carmen asked.

He shrugged. When he was finished, he pulled his finger away and leaned back, inspecting the stick figure he drew.

"What is that?"

"It's a gingerbread man, like when they get taken."

Carmen's heart jumped into her throat. "Don't say that!" She gripped the sleeve of her shirt in her palm and wiped the fog off the window completely, then she grabbed her little brother by the wrist and dragged him into the living room. "Come on," she said.

They had turned on just about every light in the house to assuage their fear, but it didn't seem to help at all; because even as the light illuminated and basked every object in every room, it created a multitude of shadows behind every wall and piece of furniture.

The two of them stood in the kitchen, leaning against the counter and just silently looking at each other for a while. They didn't know what to do; there was nothing they wanted to do. Tommy tried reading his book for a while, but his hands became jittery. Carmen felt like she was waiting on pins and needles for some kind of news.

"We should help look for him," Tommy suggested.

Carmen shook her head sternly. "No."

"But what if it was me?"

This got Carmen angry, and she couldn't help her eyes squeezing out fresh, hot tears. She stepped forward and covered his mouth with her hand. "It's not going to be you, okay?" She relieved the pressure a moment later, realizing how much she was squeezing his mouth, and she sunk down and wrapped her arms around him. "Everything's gonna be fine, you hear me?"

Tommy nodded.

When she composed herself, she stood up and suggested they sit on the couch and turn on the TV for noise. They did so, and as they tried to flip the channels, they were both distracted by their wayward thoughts. It was like an itch that crept under their skin and caused them agony from the inside; it was the mystery that they just had to know more of. Carmen flipped to the local news.

A reporter was standing in the street, interviewing a neighbor of Mrs. Darton. Carmen and Tommy quickly realized that they'd shown it already and this was just a repeat. There must have been no new information. After the regurgitated interview ended, it went back to the local newsroom where the anchors talked about the case.

"Hold on a minute," one of them said, holding his finger to his earpiece. "We're just getting word now that a new clue has been discovered in the case at the site of the disappearance. We're taking you there now." The two anchors stared blankly toward the camera, waiting for the feed to switch over.

Carmen and Tommy leaned forward on the couch.

The feed finally cut over to a familiar female reporter standing in front of the bright glow from the camera. Darkened woods stood behind her, and every time she spoke, a tiny white cloud escaped her lips from the cold.

"Hi Tom, we are back here at the spot where Jeremy Darton was last seen. He disappeared at around 8:10 this evening, leaving behind one of his shoes and a gingerbread man cookie that his mother said she had no idea how he got. But now a new clue has been discovered by police that they first overlooked, and they're allowing us to show it to you tonight."

The woman turned and stepped across the shallow gash running through the backyard to the start of the tree line on the other side as the camera followed her. The view bumped and jostled until they were both across and the woman turned and stood next to a tree, holding the microphone up to her mouth.

"A carving has been found etched into this tree, right in front of where Jeremy disappeared."

The reporter pointed to it, and the camera zoomed in.

"Now, it appears to be some kind of symbol that looks like a lasso or a noose. It's about six inches long, and Dorothy Darton says she's never seen it here before tonight. We don't want to speculate much until the facts come in, but it's possible that we could be looking at some kind of copycat emulating the disappearance of David Basham three years ago, and some police suggest that this symbol could be a calling card."

— CHAPTER FIVE —

A Hundred Smiling Pumpkins

Carmen and Tommy sat on the couch and the TV droned in the background. Their eyes stared at it, but they weren't actually seeing anything; their minds had gone blank with a buzz of noise about the boy's disappearance, and questions filled every mental doorway they had.

Carmen's cell phone went off and buzzed on the table.

She jumped. When the shock wore off, she leaned forward and snatched it up. "Oh crap."

"What?" Tommy asked.

"I totally forgot... I was supposed to go to Breanna's house and pick up her part of the assignment we're handing in tomorrow in class." She thought for a moment, then texted back.

Can you drop it off at my house?
No. My parents have the car
I can't leave the house right now. Can you bring it over?
Sorry, I don't want to go out by myself right now with what happened...

Carmen groaned and leaned her elbow on the top of the couch.

"What's wrong?" Tommy asked.

She looked at him. "Breanna's uncle is picking her up first thing tomorrow morning to go to her family's cottage, but I forgot that her parents are already there with the car. She's not going to be in class tomorrow to hand in the assignment with me, so I was supposed to pick it up from her house today."

"Can't you pick it up in the morning?"

She shook her head. "No, she's leaving really early. I have to get it tonight."

"So let's get it," he said.

Carmen sat back, defeated. What choice did she have? The assignment was worth fifteen percent of her mark. But her father made her promise that she and her brother wouldn't leave the house again tonight. She could leave her brother home alone while she ran out quickly and got it, but he was only nine, and if anything happened to him while she was gone...

"Well?" Tommy said. He leaned forward expectantly, like he was ready to go on an adventure, despite the one he just came back from.

Carmen looked at him with a flash of fire in her eyes. "If you tell Dad, I'll kill you, deal?"

Her threat didn't seem to faze him as he jovially nodded his head up and down.

She made sure they were both bundled up for the cold, then she stood at the front door, holding it open a crack and peering out into the night.

"What are you waiting for?" Tommy said impatiently from behind her.

She pulled back from the door. "Nothing." She opened it and reluctantly stepped out of the house. They took a similar route to the one she had taken on the way to the school. Breanna's house wasn't far from there, and they would need to head through downtown to get there. There were less cars driving by on the roads now, and as they got close to the main streets, they saw fewer people walking around. Stores would be closing soon, and everyone who didn't still have business to do was probably safely hunkered in their homes or out searching for Jeremy.

A gust of wind picked up as they hurried down Forester Street, and this one seemed to cut through their clothes. Tommy shivered. Carmen looked around, expecting an owl to be staring at her or some strange sensation to befall them.

"Do you hear that?" Carmen asked, stopping suddenly.

"Hear what?"

A gentle breeze rumbled through a set of bushes lining the edge of a park next to them. Tree branches swayed from side to side, and the soft buzzing of bugs' wings hitting streetlights drifted through the air. A car horn honked briefly about half a mile away.

Carmen glanced around. She couldn't put her finger on it, but something was wrong. She gripped her brother's hand, squeezing it too tightly.

"Ow!" he cried.

But she didn't hear him. The darkness encapsulated them, and Carmen realized that they were standing in a patch of shadow between streetlights. She pulled her brother forward, finding refuge in the muted glow.

A scampering of little feet near the bushes. A flap of a bird's wings overhead. The creak of a stop sign as a stiff wind twisted it.

Tommy peered into the dark. Outside the protection of the streetlight, it was nearly pitch-black—abnormally so.

There was a thin space between the bottom of the bushes and the ground at the edge of the park that was shrouded in opaque shadow. Carmen felt something from there, almost as if the darkness and the cold emanated from the space.

A flash of glowing eyes appeared in the black.

Carmen jumped.

The stray cat cried and ran out of the bushes, darting down the street.

What was going on? Carmen couldn't figure it out. And whether he was influenced by her agitation or not, Tommy started to feel uneasy, too. He felt the pressure relieve from his hand as Carmen calmed down, and he took a deep breath.

"Let's go," Carmen said suddenly, not wanting to linger any longer.

Tommy turned back to the direction they were heading in from looking at the cat, and out of the corner of his eye he saw something streak by above him. He looked up.

It was out of sight now, but for a second, he swore he saw something fly by in front of the full moon. It didn't look like a bird or anything else of the sort. It almost seemed like... a person. But that was impossible... wasn't it?

He gulped. "I think I saw—"

"Let's go!" she repeated frantically. She pulled on his arm harder and this time his legs were forced into motion. They moved down the street almost in a jog and came up to Rosedale. And though they moved closer to civilization, the heavy, negative feeling plaguing Carmen didn't go away; it was like a cloak of foreboding hung heavy on her shoulders.

In the distance, away from downtown, she could see high-powered flashlights cutting through the darkness in a faraway stretch of woods. "Jeremy!" could faintly be heard above the swell of the wind. But Carmen tried to stop paying attention to her surroundings anymore, adopting a tunnel vision along the path toward Breanna's house.

They cut through the town square in the middle of downtown, and there were still a few people walking around. Most of the stores had already closed up for the night, but a few were still open. They passed a few townsfolk they recognized, and they exchanged a brief hello, though Carmen could tell the looks on all of their faces were strained for some reason.

When they arrived at Breanna's house, the two of them huddled close to the front door as Carmen knocked. She looked over her shoulder at the dark and didn't see anyone else in sight. If someone was prowling around, waiting to snatch someone up, this would be the place to do it.

The door swung open and Carmen backed up with a gasp.

"Oh, sorry," Breanna said. She grabbed something off a table next to the door and held it out to her.

"It's okay, thanks," Carmen said. She took the clipped stack of papers from Breanna and held them tightly to her chest. "Sorry for being late today."

"It's no problem. I'm just glad you could make it. Pretty crazy what's going on, huh?"

"Yeah."

"I'm almost sad to be going to the cottage for the weekend. It would be kinda preoccupying not knowing what's happening here."

"I'm sure they'll find him," Carmen said, though in the moment she didn't mean her words at all.

Breanna's hands were clinging tightly to the edge of the door, and Carmen saw an uneasy look on her face. "Well, bye," she said hastily, and she slammed the door shut.

Carmen and Tommy took a step back, surprised.

"What was that about?" he asked.

"I don't know," Carmen replied, staring at the door. Something strange was going on in this town, and she thought that it had something more to do than just with the little boy's disappearance. She turned. "Come on, we gotta get back before dad knows we're gone."

They traced their way back, cutting through downtown to get home, and when they reached the center of it, they heard a rumbling of voices and saw a waving of lights in the distance.

Down the street, coming from the wooded residential areas, a crowd of townspeople marched in their direction. Some of the group broke off onto other streets, but the majority of them carried on toward the town square. Various members of the crowd shouted Jeremy's name as they searched around in every nook and cranny.

Carmen shrunk back, fearing that their father would be in the crowd and spot them. She pulled Tommy into the doorway of a nearby shop, peeking around the corner at the approaching group.

A car slowly rolled up the street, pulling to a stop by the curb next to them. The window rolled down.

It took Carmen a few moments to realize that it had, then she slowly turned and saw her father sitting in his police cruiser, staring at her and Tommy. His face was painted with his displeasure.

Her mouth fell open, trying to sort through the words to say in her defense.

The search party entered the town square and suddenly all of the streetlights flickered. Everyone stopped and looked around. Then the lights went out completely.

Darkness surrounded them from every direction, and the only illumination came from their flashlights. Murmurs rippled through the dark, and a growing sense of fear permeated them.

One of the townspeople shrieked.

Everyone spread out in a panic, trying to figure out what had caused the shock.

Glowing orange lights appeared in the middle of the square. They came in strange, crazed shapes, like leering, taunting faces. They lit up one right after the other in rapid succession until a huge pile of glowing orange eyes stared at the townspeople. The beams of their flashlights illuminated the pile and they gasped at the enormity of it. A small mountain of carved jack-o'-lanterns with evil and demented faces filled the square.

Robert's jaw dropped from inside the cruiser.

Fear clutched the townspeople, and bad memories of surrounding the old woman's house on the hill with jack-o'-lanterns haunted them.

"It's the witch!" someone shrieked. A man ran out in front of the others at the edge of the square, thrusting his arm toward the pile of jack-o'-lanterns. "She's back!"

The townspeople shrunk away in fear at his words. They were illogical, because the woman had been innocent, and they all knew that. And now she was dead. But all the same, his words clung to their fearful, primitive hearts.

"And she didn't just take Jeremy!" the man cried. "She's going to take *all* of our children!"

— CHAPTER SIX —

JAIL TALK

Carmen cut off the crust on Tommy's sandwich, then she put the knife in the sink. "Come on, you're going to be late for school!" she yelled.

A few seconds later, heavy footsteps came charging down the hallway to the front of the house. "I'm ready!" Tommy exclaimed. He was already dressed up in his coat, his boots, and he had his backpack slung over his shoulders.

"Impressive response time," Carmen said. She wrapped up the sandwich in saran wrap and put it in his Iron Man lunchbox, closing it up and stuffing it into his backpack for him. She grabbed her own backpack and her purse, then she put on her shoes and coat. "Ready to go?"

"Yep," Tommy replied.

She opened the door and the cold air of the morning greeted them, and though the ominous night was gone, the feeling still remained, like something was off. They still hadn't found little Jeremy through the night, to her knowledge, and she wondered how the townspeople would react today in the sobering morning light.

But Tommy didn't seem to be phased; no matter what happened, his boundless optimism shone through, and he seemed oblivious to the world around him as he skipped along the sidewalk to the bus stop. Carmen stood by his side and waited for the bus to pick him up before she took a city bus to the college. Sometimes their father would give Tommy a ride to school if the timing worked out, or sometimes he would wait with him for the bus to pick him up, but those occasions seemed to be getting rarer these days.

Time seemed to pass at a crawl, and Carmen glanced up and down the road for the school bus. She checked the time on her phone.

"It should be here by now, shouldn't it?" Tommy said, looking up at her.

Carmen frowned. "Yeah, it's already 8:45. I'm going to be late."

They waited a few more minutes, but the bus still didn't show up.

"What do we do?" Tommy asked.

"Come on," she said, thinking of something. She took his arm and pulled him up the street. "We'll take a city bus. There should be one hitting the stop at Rosedale in a minute or two." They jogged along the sidewalk for a couple blocks until they got to the bus stop. Cars rolled by on the road, and in the distance behind the sporadic line they could see the tall and lumbering bus rolling down the street. It stopped next to them and opened its doors, and Carmen and Tommy climbed into it.

She said hi to the driver, but he only gave her an unimpressed look. Carmen furrowed her brow and reached into her pocket for some change. She sorted through a handful of coins and dropped the correct fare in the slot and turned to the aisle with her brother.

The bus was half-filled, and all of them seemed to be in a glum mood. Carmen didn't blame them considering the circumstances, but it seemed to be something more than that; there was just a general sense of malaise and irritation etched into most of their faces. They both tried nodding or saying hello to some of them, but they didn't get anything more than a terse nod back.

They sat down in an empty row by the back doors as the bus lurched forward and sped down the road. Looking out the window, it seemed like a normal day in the town with everyone going to work or running errands. When the bus came up to the intersection on Rosedale and Forester, Carmen pulled the stop request cord and the bus screeched to an abrupt halt.

As they got up, Carmen yelled her thanks to the driver. Glaring eyes were all she saw on the rearview mirror. They left the bus and it sped off, leaving them standing in the cold and Carmen confused.

"What's wrong?" Tommy asked.

"I don't know," she said. "Do people seem a bit... off to you today?"

Tommy thought about it. "Hmm, I don't know..."

She shrugged it off and they walked down the road at a brisk pace, still a couple blocks away from the school. But as they got closer and the school came into view behind a row of tall trees, they saw a strange and unexpected sight.

A large crowd had gathered in front of the school, all marching around in a circle and holding picket signs.

"What the...?" Carmen muttered.

"Higher wages now!" someone from the crowd shouted.

"That's Mrs. Andrews!" Tommy said, pointing. "And there's my gym teacher, Mr. Weston."

"They're on strike?" Carmen said. "I never heard about teachers going on strike today."

Their signs were filled with statements demanding higher pay and better treatment. And the tone of not only their demeanor and speech, but even the way the lettering on their signs had been written and slanted, seemed aggressive.

"What's going on here?" Carmen asked one of the teachers marching by.

The older woman scowled at her. "Higher wages!" she shouted into her face.

Carmen took a shocked step back.

There were a few parents with children showing up to the school and then quickly turning around after they saw what was going on. Some of them milled about to watch the demonstration, and Carmen tried her luck with them.

"Teachers' strike," a young father told her, holding his son in front of him by the shoulders. "Citywide."

"Citywide? Like, all teachers?" Carmen asked.

The man nodded. "The college, too."

"But why all of a sudden?"

"Beats me," he said. "Enjoy your day off, I guess. Not for me though; I've got to get to work." He looked down at his son. "Now I just gotta figure out what to do with this brat for the day." The look on his face as he stared down at his son couldn't have been interpreted as anything other than anger. "Let's go," he said, yanking his son away from the crowd.

Carmen was speechless.

— — —

"Okay! Okay!" Robert called to the agitated crowd standing in the lobby of the police station. There was a good dozen and a half of them that were pushing their way forward in the small space, shouting and demanding answers. "I'm going to give a statement at noon!" he called over the ruckus. "At noon!"

His deputy and officers were holding the crowd back in front of him.

"What's being done to find him?" one man demanded.

"We've still got search parties sweeping the town!" Robert announced. "And we're going to keep them going until he's found, I promise you that!"

"That's not good enough!" the man shouted back.

Their back-and-forth struggle went on for another ten minutes until the officers finally managed to settle the crowd down enough to push them out of the station.

"Lock the doors," Robert said to Don.

"But Boss..."

"Lock 'em!" he snarled. "Just for fifteen minutes, so we can all clear our heads."

Don nodded, looking at the chief carefully, then he went to the front and locked the doors. Some of the crowd outside was still loitering, a few peering through the glass suspiciously at the officers.

Robert retreated to his office, plunking down into his chair and leaning on the desk, resting his forehead against the surface. His head was pounding; he had a headache all morning.

His phone began ringing. The sounds of more phones ringing drifted through the hallway.

He sighed, then he reached over and picked it up. "Yeah? Uh huh. Not yet." He slammed it down.

The phone rang again.

He looked at it with a hateful eye, then he turned his head away and ignored it.

Don spoke on the phone in the lobby to someone reporting a robbery. He took down notes, then he looked up quickly when he heard banging on the front doors of the station.

Carmen and Tommy had worked their way through the crowd and slapped on the glass after pulling on the doors and finding them locked.

Don held up a finger telling them to wait while he finished up his call. He put the phone down and walked over to them, unlocking the doors. "What are you guys doing here?" he asked the kids as they came in.

"School's canceled," Carmen said.

"The teachers are on strike!" Tommy added.

"On strike?" Don was confused. He hadn't heard about this.

The two of them walked down the hallway to their father's office. Carmen knocked on the door and saw him groggily rouse from his rest on the desk. Strangely, he didn't seem surprised to see them. His face looked tired, like he hadn't gotten sleep in a week.

"Hey," he said simply.

"Are you all right?" Carmen asked, concerned.

He grumbled something that was close to a yes as he rubbed the back of his neck. "Neck's killing me for some reason, but otherwise I'm fine. Why aren't you in school?"

"All the teachers are on strike," Carmen said.

Before he could react, he rubbed his neck more vigorously, squeezing his eyes shut like he was in pain.

"Are you sure you're okay, Dad?" Carmen asked, stepping around the desk to him.

"I'm fine, Sweetpea," he said, lifting her hand and kissing the back of it. "Don't you worry."

The phone rang.

Robert just stared at it.

"Are you going to answer it?" Tommy asked.

He grumbled. "Ughh, I better..." He reluctantly leaned forward and snatched the phone off the cradle. He said hello, then he pressed it against his chest and looked at his kids. "Look, I'm real busy here today. Carmen,

Sweetie, why don't you take your brother somewhere for the day? It's probably going to be a late day for me."

She nodded. "Yeah, sure."

"Just make sure you stay safe. Don't go anywhere by yourselves."

Carmen agreed, and Tommy looked at his father as he turned his attention to the phone call. Tommy thought of going up and hugging him, telling him that he missed him, but as he saw his father pour his attention into the phone call and not give him a second glance, he faltered, then he turned for the door.

Carmen lingered, watching her dad take the call. Like everyone else in the town this morning, he just didn't seem quite right. She had to admit that she felt a bit off herself, and she had remembered how everyone reacted when David went missing three years ago, but this was different.

The front doors of the station opened again and the crowd pushed their way back in. "Hey!" Don shouted as all the officers mobilized to get them out.

Robert looked up at the open doorway to the hall. "I gotta go," he announced into the phone, then he dropped it and bolted to his feet. He rushed into the hallway, holding up his hands and shouting.

Carmen glanced around for her brother and realized he was gone. She peeked out into the lobby, but there was no one aside from the crowd and the officers. "Tommy!" she shouted, looking down the other end of the hall. The corridor stretched past rows of offices and rounded a corner to the jail cells in the back. There were only about a dozen of them in total—a small jail—but they were usually enough for such a small town. Still, she feared the idea of her brother back there by himself and thought that he must have slipped out the front door and was waiting for her outside.

But when she rounded the corner and saw her brother standing not only in front of the jail cells, but standing right up to the bars of the farthest one, wrapping his hands around them and pressing his face between them, her heart jumped in her chest.

"*Tommy!*" she said sharply. "Get away from there!"

He turned his head to her. "But I'm just talking to my friend."

Carmen rushed to him, passing one or two people locked up and lying on their cots. She wrenched Tommy away from the bars and squeezed his shoulders, staring fiercely into his eyes. "Just what do you think you're doing!"

Tommy looked upset, opening his mouth and trying to find an answer. He didn't think he was doing anything wrong. The man seemed nice enough, after all.

"Sorry, I didn't mean to scare you," the man inside the jail cell said.

She turned and looked in it.

"I was just talking to your brother about the witch."

"Witch? What witch?"

"It's her, I'm telling you!" he said, agitation filling his voice. "She took Jeremy."

"That was you..." Carmen said. "In the town square last night."

He leaned against the cement wall behind his cot. "That's why they locked me up. The chief said I was causing a panic and making the townspeople scared. But I don't care! I have to warn them! The only problem is they don't want to listen."

The man was thin and shabbily dressed. His short hair was a mess, and his face had an unhealthy thinness to it. Still, the way he spoke suggested that he was sensible enough.

"Come on," Carmen said to her little brother, ushering him away from the cell.

"She might take your brother next," the man called from behind them.

Anger boiled in the pit of Carmen's stomach. She marched back to the cell, grabbing the bars herself this time. She pointed a finger at the man. "Hey, you listen to me, buddy! Don't ever say that in front of my brother again, you hear me?"

"I didn't mean to offend," he said softly. "But another child is going to go missing at any moment. And then another one after that."

The man got under her skin. She shouldn't have been so fascinated about what he was saying, but she was. "How do you know all this? You're talking about the woman who lived on the hill, right? The one that got burned? Well, she's dead."

The man shook his head vigorously, and the certainty in his face frightened her. "No," he said, "far from it."

Carmen tried to say something else, but she choked on her words.

"The gingerbread cookie. The pumpkins. The shoe. It's recreating itself. Everyone has to protect themselves—protect their *children*—before it's too late."

Tommy stared at the man in fascination.

"But..." Carmen started. "But she didn't take that kid three years ago. She was innocent; he just got lost. I know all the kids around here thought she was a witch, but there's no such thing as an actual witch. And most importantly... she's *dead*."

"Just promise me one thing," he said.

"What?" Carmen asked.

"When they locked me up last night, they took all my things. They'll let me out in a few hours, probably, but there's one thing they took that you could probably use more than I can right now. Do you know where they keep the items they take from people?"

"Yeah," Carmen said. "What's in there?"

"There's something that looks like a necklace. But it's a lot more than that. The cord has a smooth rose-colored stone hanging from it. Put it on your brother and make him wear it at all times."

"What's going on here?" Carmen asked, exasperated.

He leaned forward. "The witch is back. She didn't take that boy three years ago, but the townspeople thought she did, and it cost her her life. Now she's getting her revenge. And she won't stop until all the children are hers, including Tommy."

— CHAPTER SEVEN —

INFERNO

"How did he know your name?" Carmen demanded.

"I told him," Tommy said. "His name's Peter. He says he's lived here all his life."

"You shouldn't be talking to strangers like that, especially ones in jail." She was angry with him, but she couldn't help but be fascinated by the man. She turned the necklace over in her hands, letting the rose-colored stone glint off the sunlight as they walked home.

"He wasn't going to hurt anyone," Tommy argued. "Besides, he wants to protect us from the witch."

Carmen scoffed. "What the heck is this thing, anyway?"

Tommy looked at it. "Maybe it's like an amoolut."

"You mean an amulet?"

"Yeah. Maybe you can cast spells with it or something cool."

"Not likely," Carmen said, stuffing it in her pocket.

They arrived back at their house just before noon, and Carmen stuffed the necklace in a drawer in her bedroom, knowing it was nothing but junk. *He's probably crazy*, she said to herself. *Thinking there's a witch trying to get everyone. Absurd.* She shrugged and wandered around the house, trying to figure out what to do. She looked at the assignment sitting on the kitchen counter that she and Breanna had put so much time into and sighed. She hadn't expected to stay home today, and now she didn't know what to do with herself.

Tommy wandered off to his room and played with his action figures. No one could ever catch him being bored, as he could find adventures in the simplest things.

After making three rounds through the house, absentmindedly checking her phone here and there, Carmen finally plunked on the couch and turned on the TV. There was still no word on Jeremy, but she knew her father would be giving a statement at noon on the local news. She flipped to the news channel and saw a reporter standing in the town square.

The same female from the night before was standing in front of the camera holding her microphone, and in the background behind her, two men were clearing the last of the jack-o'-lanterns that had been mysteriously placed there in the night.

Carmen leaned forward and squinted her eyes.

"Just now, as the city is clearing the last of this bizarre scene," the reporter said to the camera, "a strange symbol has been discovered underneath the pile." The camera zoomed over her shoulder, focusing on something painted across the bricks of the town square, maybe twelve or fifteen feet wide. "This mysterious symbol was discovered after the jack-o'-lanterns had started to be removed, and it's unclear who put it here or what it represents, but as you can see it appears to most closely resemble a broadcast tower. What it means is a mystery to everyone, but it's safe to say that whoever put it here, also placed the jack-o'-lanterns. The city has tried to power wash the symbol off the bricks, but so far it isn't coming off yet, leading police to investigate what material it's made of and where it could have come from."

"What's that?" Tommy asked.

Carmen was startled, not knowing her brother had snuck up on her. She looked over her shoulder. "It's from those pumpkins last night. Just like that carving they found on the tree..." She had no idea what it all meant.

Tommy made a quiet, amused sound, like he found all of this fascinating, then he walked around the couch and joined his sister.

In a few minutes, the camera feed cut over to outside the front of the police station, and their father was standing at a podium with a few microphones pointed up at his mouth. His deputy, Don, was standing next to him, and a couple other officers could be seen in the shot. Camera flashes washed over him as he looked at the gathering just off camera and made his announcement.

"Good afternoon, everyone," he said. "I'm making a quick statement here to update you on everything that's going on with the disappearance of Jeremy Darton. As of this moment, we still haven't found him and we don't have any leads as to his whereabouts. I would like to remind all of you to stay calm in this time as we continue to search for him; as we all know very well, panic will do us no good." His face fell in a somber expression as he stared down at the podium and composed his thoughts. "Halloween is two days away, and I would like to remind everyone that despite Jeremy's disappearance, it is perfectly safe to take your kids out trick-or-treating, and the police department encourages it."

Tommy straightened up on the couch, his eyes turning plate-sized in excitement.

But Carmen scrunched her eyebrows in suspicion.

"So for now," Robert continued, "it is our advice that everyone should go about their normal business. The police are still patrolling this town and will keep its citizens safe. Everything is under control, and we're sure that Jeremy will be found soon. Thank you."

Reporters off-camera shouted a litany of questions, but all of it was just white noise to Carmen. She couldn't believe her father said that in light of what was happening; she certainly remembered three years ago when she tried to take her brother trick-or-treating and he'd come home with no more than half a dozen pieces of candy in his bag. And now another child was missing, and it was business as usual? It didn't make any sense.

"All right!" Tommy exclaimed. "I get to go trick-or-treating!" He kneeled on the couch and turned to his sister, shaking her shoulder. "Can we go get a costume? Can we go get a costume?!"

She ignored her brother. There was something off about their father in his statement... not just what he said, but the way he spoke. That same heaviness that seemed to weigh on him in the station earlier was still there. But she couldn't put her finger on it, and she couldn't come up with a better word than simply... *strange*.

― ― ―

The hallways were dark and the school was empty, except for one person.

The janitor walked through a hallway on the ground floor. His footsteps clapped on the cement and echoed across the bare walls. He moved from classroom to classroom, mopping the floors. Darkness had fallen outside, and he only kept the lights on he needed as he moved through the school, turning them on and off as he came and went. Short strips of illumination filled whatever section he was currently in, leaving the rest of the school blacked out.

The school was silent. Even as he walked by the windows in each classroom to clean, it seemed like the breeze outside was inaudible; no car horns or engines revving could be heard in the distance; there were no children playing outside or people walking around. It was like he was the last man on Earth.

He finished mopping the floor of the principal's office and stepped out into the hallway, dropping the mop in the bucket and wiping a thin layer of sweat off his forehead.

A faint clicking sound came from somewhere in the darkness.

The janitor stopped and looked around. "Hello?" he called out. He strained his ears and listened.

Silence.

He shrugged and pulled the mop and bucket along the floor. The wheels were old and squeaky, and a high-pitched whine echoed through the school as he walked. He passed a door then stopped, hearing that same clicking noise over the whine of the wheels.

He turned around and stared into the dark.

"What is that?" he muttered under his breath.

He left the bucket and took a few steps forward, stopping in front of the door that he just passed. It was the one that led down to the basement. He leaned and pressed his ear to it. The clicking was louder.

He opened the door and its hinges groaned. It was so silent in the school that he could hear a pin drop from any part of it. He flicked on the light switch next to him to illuminate the stairwell, but the light bulb didn't come on. He looked up and grumbled under his breath. He patted his pockets, but realized that he didn't have his flashlight on him. It was in the basement.

The clicking sound continued, drifting up from somewhere down below.

He gripped the railing tightly and started down the stairs, his heart beating faster than it should have. He moved slowly, his old bones doing him no favors. When he rounded the corner halfway down the stairs, he took his time with the rest of them, and when he made it to the bottom he used his hands to feel out the walls in the dark.

It was pitch-black, and he couldn't see a thing. He knew the flashlight was down here, but he couldn't remember where. His fingers glided along the cold wall and found the light switch. He flicked it on. The bulb didn't light up. His heart lurched.

The absolute silence of the school upstairs carried on down here, save for the mysterious clicking somewhere ahead of him. He could hear his own breathing getting heavier, and then as he cleared a wall in front of him, he saw a dim orange glow coming from the right. It was from the fire burning in the furnace.

The clicking came from the same direction. He carefully rounded the corner into the little room that housed the furnace and some other piping, and he stood before it as the orange glow outlined the hatch in the front of it.

The clicking slowed down, but increased in volume. Now it sounded like someone was hammering on the furnace door from the inside.

"*What the hell?*" he muttered. He stepped forward slowly, and he couldn't understand why, but his heart was thumping madly in his chest now. If there was something wrong with the furnace, he would fix it, and the situation didn't account for his childlike fear that he was experiencing. The light danced in the darkness, and his eyes were wide, like he expected the furnace to gobble him up at any moment. He pictured the door creaking open, giving way to the inviting flame. Hands of fire would stretch out and seductively wrap themselves around him, pulling him into the blaze. Sweat dripped down his forehead now as he walked, mesmerized by the orange light.

Click. Click. *Click!*

He stood right in front of the furnace. It exploded.

The door was ripped off with incredible force, and it clipped him in the shoulder, tearing a huge gash out of it. A wave of flame rushed out and engulfed him.

The janitor stumbled back into the other section of the basement, completely covered in flames. He screamed and waved his hands in the air like a madman. He slammed into a wall in front of him, but he couldn't feel it behind the excruciating pain. His screams filled the entire school, but no one was there to hear them.

His towering inferno of a figure stumbled through the darkness like a demon from Hell until his screams were choked out of him and he fell to his knees, finally collapsing on the floor, dead.

Some small pockets of fire danced on the walls of the small furnace room, and they quickly shrank and were snuffed out. And left behind, in a black scorch on the wall, was another symbol, this one resembling a heart dripping blood with a dagger plunged through it.

— CHAPTER EIGHT —

A TASTY GIFT

After a long evening at work, Robert had enough time to go home and have dinner with his children before he had to go back to the station. He put his deputy and all of his officers on overtime, and they were all working around the clock to not only find the missing boy, but to quell the rising tide of panic that had swept through the town from his disappearance.

The three of them ate dinner in relative silence. Both Carmen and Tommy could tell that their father wasn't his normal self, even compared to when he had been overworked in the past. He seemed distant; detached.

"So... I can go trick-or-treating?" Tommy asked.

Robert looked up from his meal at his son. His jaw chewed slowly, and he didn't say anything. He looked back down and continued eating.

Carmen reached under the table and grabbed her brother's hand, giving it a soft squeeze. She knew he was too young to understand what was going on with their father. She barely knew herself, but this kind of sudden change in him was frightening for a nine-year-old.

"You... you said everyone could go trick-or-treating, right?" Tommy asked timidly. He began to second-guess himself, like he hadn't heard his father's statement correctly on the news.

"No," Robert said at last. "You're not going anywhere."

"But—"

Robert slammed his fist down on the table, causing the plates to jump and rattle. Carmen and Tommy jumped in their seats. Robert squeezed his eyes shut and pressed his fingers to them, trying to alleviate the pressure behind them. Mostly hidden behind his hand, Carmen could see his lips peel open and his teeth grating against each other.

She reached out and softly placed a hand on his. "Dad?"

The tension seemed to wash out of him and he looked up at her. "What is it, Sweetpea?" he asked. The bizarre strain and heaviness in his eyes a moment ago seemed to be gone, and now there was a softness in them.

"Are you okay?"

"I'm fine." He rubbed his hand on the back of his neck, then he shoveled another bite of pork into his mouth. He chewed and swallowed it, then he looked at Tommy. "Of course you can go trick-or-treating, Kiddo."

Tommy slowly leaned back in his seat, like he was growing suspicious of his father like Carmen had. "What? Are you sure?"

"Of course," Robert said. "We've got the city well protected. No one else is going to disappear on our watch." He gave a smile to his kids, but it was counterfeit. He set down his fork and rubbed the back of his neck again more vigorously.

"Can you take me to get a costume?" Tommy asked. "I can go with Carmen if you're too busy..."

Robert's eyes squeezed shut again and he bared his teeth very clearly now for both of them to see. "No!" he shouted. He slammed his fist on the table again, then he picked up his plate and hurled it across the room. Carmen and Tommy both ducked in fear as the plate shattered against the wall and food splattered everywhere. He stood up suddenly and paced to the kitchen.

The phone rang.

He snatched it up so quickly that his kids thought it was going to launch out of his hand and fly through the window.

"What?" he asked. He nodded, listening along, then he hung up the phone. He grabbed his coat and headed for the front door, telling his kids that something happened at the school and he had to go check it out in a barely-intelligible mumble.

And in the next moment, he was gone, leaving Carmen and Tommy sitting at the dining room table, stunned.

Tommy slowly got up, walking over to the broken plate to clean it up.

"Don't touch that," Carmen told him. "I'll get it." She went to the kitchen and grabbed a dustpan and some paper towels, then she knelt down on the floor in the mess and began cleaning up. Tommy stood over her shoulder and offered to help, but she dismissed him. "Go to your room," she said.

Fearing anger from her as well, Tommy did as she said and disappeared down the hallway.

Carmen quietly sobbed as she cleaned up her father's mess, not understanding what was happening and what had gotten into him. When it was cleaned up and she had calmed down a little, she walked to Tommy's room and knocked on the door. He told her to come in and she leaned in the doorway.

"Hey, don't let all that worry you," she said. But she could see she was unconvincing.

"Yeah, whatever," Tommy replied. He lay in his cubbyhole, reading his Hardy Boys book. But as Carmen stood and watched him, it was clear that his eyes weren't moving and he was blankly staring at the page, deep in thought. He spoke up at last. "What's wrong with Dad?"

"Nothing's wrong with him," she said, trying to cover for him. "He's just under a lot of stress lately. You have to understand that he went through all this three years ago, and now that it's happening again. I think it's a bit too much for him." She didn't believe herself, but she was trying to say anything to make her brother feel better.

"So will you take me to get a costume?" he asked quietly.

"What? Tommy, no. It's too dangerous out there this year."

"Because of the witch?"

"No. There's no witch. That guy was just saying something to get a rise out of you."

"Get a what?"

"Never mind. But maybe next year when things settle down."

Tears welled up in his eyes. His bottom lip stretched out into a pout. He wasn't faking it; this was genuine.

"Don't cry."

"I miss Mom," he said suddenly.

Carmen was stunned for a moment. "I... I miss her too. I think about her every day. Do you?"

He nodded.

"Well do you think she would want to see you sad like this?"

He shook his head. "I think she'd want to see me happy. I think she'd want me to go trick-or-treating."

A swell of conflicting emotions rose up in Carmen's chest. They were guilt, shock, love, anger, fear, and many others. Mostly she was surprised at how deftly he had just played his cards. "You're good, you know that?"

He looked up at her with the most pathetic eyes she'd ever seen. "Are you saying you'll take me?"

Carmen glanced at the crack of the window visible between his curtains and the darkness through it. She hesitated, wrestling with the last vestiges of resistance in her, but then at last she could do nothing but relent to him. "Fine," she said. "I'll take you this year. If there's any one giving out candy, we'll get you some, and we'll stick to the main areas where others are so we'll be safe.

And if nobody's giving it out, I'll get you some candy myself, does that sound good?"

Tommy wiped the tears out of his eyes. "Yeah."

"But you have to promise you won't tell Dad we're doing this. Just leave him alone for a little while—let him blow off some steam. He'll probably be busy that night anyway and won't know we're out, so just keep this between us, deal?"

He nodded. "Okay." And as if to seal the deal in making her feel as guilty as possible, he crawled out of his cubbyhole, walked across the room to her, and wrapped his arms around her, nestling his face against her chest.

A smirk crossed her face as her heart swelled, and she ran her fingers through his hair.

— — —

A little girl sat on her bed with the door to her room closed as she played with her doll. She brushed its hair with a little comb, and she twisted it around, inspecting it from all angles. When it was to her liking, she set it next to the other dolls she had. She picked up a little teacup and set it on a little table. Just above a whisper, she feigned dialogue in a high-pitched voice. Her mom was somewhere in the living room on the other end of the house, and she had plenty of time to play with her dolls before she went to bed.

Something tapped on her window.

The girl looked up. There were thin white curtains covering the window, and she could see the muted square of darkness behind them. She didn't hear anything else, so she turned her attention back to her dolls, picking up a tiny teapot and pretending to pour it into a cup.

A tap played on the glass again.

She looked up. She stared at it for a moment, and she finally decided to put the teapot down and get up. She crossed the room to the window and reached out for the curtains. The darkness loomed behind it, waiting for her to open them.

She pulled them open to each side and stared out into the night. She couldn't see anything on the other side of the glass—only her empty backyard. The blades of grass rolled gently in the breeze as the tree branches and bushes swayed. She lifted her finger and tapped on the window herself with her fingernail, mimicking the sound she'd heard. But when nothing happened, she turned around and walked back to her bed.

Tap. Tap. Tap.

The girl stopped. She slowly turned around. Regarding the window for a long time, her little feet carried her back to it. She peered outside again, but still didn't see anything in the darkness. The movement of the bushes and the trees made it look like something could have been moving around, but she couldn't spot it. Her eyes drifted along the glass, eventually falling on something sitting on the windowsill outside.

Her brow scrunched up and she placed her fingers underneath the window. She tried to lift it, but it was really heavy for her tiny size. She groaned and struggled, and the window began to budge. It went up an inch, then another, then she crouched down and pushed her palms underneath it, shoving up with all her might. The window slid up a foot, and the cold air of the dark evening floated into her bedroom.

Her mother was still in the living room, obliviously watching television.

The little girl's eyes fell on the strange object sitting on her windowsill. She reached out into the dark and grabbed it, pulling it inside. She held it up, twisting it around in her hand like she'd done with her doll and inspecting it.

It was a gingerbread man.

A smile crossed her face. She didn't know who gave it to her, but she liked the gift very much.

— CHAPTER NINE —

BLACK OUT

The motion-sensing door slid open and Carmen and Tommy walked into the store. Being in a small town like this, they didn't really have much variety, and Hugh's Grocery and Home Supply Mart was just about their one-stop-shop for all their personal needs, whether they liked it or not. They walked past the food sections and aisles toward the other end of the store where they would be able to find the seasonal Halloween costumes.

"So what do you think you want to be?" Carmen asked.

Tommy opened his mouth.

"Other than Joe Hardy," she added. "Lame costume, remember?"

His mouth closed. He walked a few paces, thinking of a retort. "Why's it a lame costume?"

"Because nobody's going to know who you are. They're just going to say, 'Oh, look, he's dressed as a boy in a red sweater. How nice.'"

Tommy grumbled under his breath.

The store was busy, with three long lines stretched from the open checkouts and a crowd of other people milling about the store.

They reached the back of the store and found a couple aisles filled with all the Halloween accessories they could want.

"You could be a pirate," Carmen offered, pulling out the premade costume.

He looked at it. "Hmm..."

She put it back on the shelf, pulling out another one. "Sailor?"

"I don't know," he said. "I don't really like it."

"Well, what do you want to be? I could put a mop on your head."

"What would that make me?"

Carmen shrugged. "I don't know... Mop Boy?"

Tommy rolled his eyes and headed down to the other end of the aisle. Carmen looked around for a little bit, then she shouted out to him, "Take a look around and find something you like. I'm just going to get a few groceries while we're here."

He turned and nodded to her, then he rounded the corner into the next aisle. There were various Halloween decorations, candy, and simple animatronics in this one, but no costumes. But standing at the end of the aisle were Brett, Randy and Shawn.

They were talking to each other quietly and laughing, then Brett pulled something off one of the shelves and stuck it inside his jacket, surreptitiously closing it and glancing around. He spotted Tommy. "Hey, what are you doing here?" he asked with a mischievous smile.

Tommy fidgeted with his fingers and slowly walked toward them. "Um, I'm looking for a Halloween costume," he replied.

"That's stupid," Brett said. "Why would you go around trick-or-treating when you can just take whatever candy you want?"

Randy glanced around, then he stretched up onto his toes and plucked a bag of candy off the shelf, slipping it into his own coat.

Tommy knew that wasn't right, but he kept quiet.

"So where's your sister?" Brett asked.

"She's getting some groceries," he said. "What are you guys doing for Halloween, then?"

Brett shrugged. "Don't know, but we'll find something fun to do. Maybe we'll break into the school now that the teachers are on strike."

Tommy swallowed. "Cool," he said. He stood upright, adjusting his posture to try to act casually and fit in, though being around Brett and the others made him awkward and nervous.

Brett laughed. "You wouldn't have the guts to break in there, anyway."

Tommy's eyes narrowed at the challenge. "I would too!"

"I bet you didn't even hear what happened there tonight," he teased.

"What?"

"Didn't think so," Brett said, laughing and turning away from him.

"Tell me!" Tommy said.

Brett turned back with a smirk. "Some janitor got wasted there."

Tommy was confused. "What do you mean?"

"He was cleaning down by the furnace in the basement and the thing exploded. The guy totally got torched."

Tommy's eyes widened. "Really?" An imagined interpretation of the event played in his head, and it horrified him.

"I heard it was the witch," Brett said.

"The one who lived in Halloween House?" Tommy asked, startled.

"Yeah, people say she didn't really die..."

"Hey, what are you guys doing?"

They all turned and saw Carmen standing at the end of the aisle. She held a small basket in her hand filled with bread, apples, and a few other things, and Brett immediately rolled his eyes.

"I saw that, you little bugger," she said. She marched down the aisle to the three of them, and Randy and Shawn gulped, but Brett stood there defiantly.

"I ain't afraid of you," Brett said.

"You will be if you talk to my brother again," she snapped back.

Tommy took a step out of the way from his sister's line of fire.

Brett turned to his friends and smacked them on the shoulder. "Come on, let's get out of here." The three of them started to move, but then Brett stopped and looked at Shawn. "Hey, you didn't take any candy."

Shawn stood awkwardly on the spot, looking between Brett and the shelf next to him.

"Do it!" Brett punched him in the shoulder this time.

A sharp breath escaped Shawn's mouth, then he quickly snatched a bag of candy off the shelf and stuffed it under his jacket as the three of them took off.

Carmen watched them go with a scornful eye, then she turned to her brother. "What did I tell you about hanging around them?"

Tommy backed up defensively. "I didn't know they were here! I just ran into them!"

She looked at him suspiciously, but she let it go. "Come on, let's get your costume and get out of here."

He followed her to the other aisle and they spent another ten minutes browsing costumes until Tommy finally settled on Spider-Man. Carmen made sure to get the right size, then she pulled it off the rack and gave it to him to carry to the checkout. They made their way up to the front and stood in line to pay for their items and get home before it got too late.

The person at the checkout ahead of them finished up and left the store, and the line shuffled forward. A card fell out of the pocket of the man standing directly in front of them.

Tommy bent down and picked it up, and went up to him and tapped on his back. "Hey mister, you dropped this."

The man turned around, a guy somewhere in his forties with short brown hair, streaked with white on the sides. He was dressed well enough, but he had a bit of a disheveled look, with rough stubble covering his face. "Oh, thanks kid," the man said as he spotted the card.

Tommy stared down at it before he extended it out to the man and saw that his name was Darius Fishburn, an advertising consultant based in Colorado. The phone number at the bottom of the card was scratched out with pen, and Tommy flipped it over to see another number scrawled on the back. He turned his attention back to the man who had his hand extended. "Oh, sorry. Here, Mr. Fishburn."

The man took his card back. "Just Simon is fine," he said.

"You're not from around here, are you?" Tommy asked."

Carmen nudged him in the side. "Tommy, it's not polite to pry."

Simon chuckled. "That's all right. No, I don't live here. I'm just passing through."

"Where are you going?" Tommy asked.

"Good question," Simon replied. "Well, I just came back from a pro bono gig at a house in Vermont, and now I'm heading to..." He pulled out a small notebook from his jacket, flipping it open and reading from it. "...Jasper, Louisiana."

"What's there?"

"Pray you never find out, kid," he said, then he smiled and rustled Tommy's hair. The line behind him emptied out and the cashier waited for him. He turned to pay for his items, and as he did, Carmen and Tommy saw a wide bandage that stretched up and wrapped over his shoulder under the collar of his shirt, like he had sustained some kind of injury.

The man paid for his items and left, and the cashier turned to the two of them and offered them a welcoming smile. Carmen ushered her brother forward and the two of them started to raise their items onto the conveyor belt.

Then the power went out.

The whole store was plunged into blackness, and frightened murmurs coursed through the crowd standing in all the lines and shopping around the store.

The front of the place was plate glass, which let in a little light from the streetlights by the road outside, but suddenly even that illumination seemed to dim as an intangible darkness settled over the entire area.

Carmen felt around for her brother, but she couldn't find him. "Tommy?" He didn't answer, and she stumbled around in the dark. She felt someone and groped them, and the other person let out a shocked cry in a clear adult voice. "Oh, sorry!" Carmen said. She moved past them. "Tommy!"

There was noise at the front of the store, like the cashiers had been fiddling around, trying to figure out what to do. Footsteps clapped through the dark, then a voice, loud and authoritative, pierced the darkness. "Sorry folks! It seems we're experiencing some kind of power outage. We're going to try to find some flashlights so everyone can safely find their way to the front."

Carmen moved through the darkness toward the back of the store, crouching down and feeling around for her little brother. She couldn't find him anywhere, and finally she stopped and listened.

The darkness blanketed her completely. It was more than just the lights being out; it was an actual oppressive feeling, similar to what she experienced before on her way to the school the previous night. It was like there was something in the darkness, watching her. She couldn't see it, she couldn't hear it, but she could feel it. Her mind immediately went to the witch that the man in the jail cell warned her about. It was a completely irrational thought, but in a time like this, rationality had no dominion.

She felt the thing in the dark lurk and creep around, and a terrible fear rose in her chest that it wanted her brother.

"Tommy!"

"Carmen?" a voice returned at last.

A beam of light appeared at the front of the store and cut through the dark. Carmen looked over her shoulder and saw it wash past her, then she turned her gaze and saw it highlight someone a dozen paces away from her in a brief flash. It was her brother.

Tommy!" she rushed over to him, moving carefully in the darkness as the flashlight swept somewhere else. They called out, relying on each other's voices to close in on one another, then Carmen reached out and found his wrist. "Tommy!" she said desperately.

"It's me!" he said, and she could hear fear in his voice, too.

"Come on, let's get out of here," she said, dragging him toward the source of the waving lights. The crowd bunched up in front of them, and Carmen tried to push and get through, feeling the dark presence lurking behind her. She didn't know what physical sense her body employed to tell that it was closing in on her, but she knew it was. It gnawed at her like an itch on the inside that she couldn't scratch, and it was making her brain go crazy. She had to get out of here. She had to get out of here now. She wrenched on her brother's arm hard, and he let out a cry of pain as he was pulled through the dense crowd. She kept an iron grip on his wrist, not willing to let him go for anything. Her ribs crashed into the dull corner of the checkout counter, and she grunted, but kept moving.

The store manager was at the front with the other cashiers, waving their flashlights around and calling out directions to the patrons. His voice was calm and soothing, but Carmen took no chances, rushing past him with her brother and heading for the exit. The automatic doors didn't work without power, but someone who'd already gone ahead of them had pried them open, and Carmen and her brother slipped out into the night.

She stumbled forward and twisted around, facing the store, her lungs heaving as she panted for breath.

"What's the matter?" Tommy asked her. "Why are you so worked up?" He looked down at his wrist in the dim light of a nearby streetlamp, rubbing the skin where she had roughly jerked it.

She didn't say anything, just regaining her breath at first as she stared at the entrance and exit of the store with wide and suspicious eyes. She was waiting for that intangible black and terrible thing to come out of there and attack them, but nothing ever did. Had she imagined it all? After all, she hadn't really seen or heard anything in the first place. But it was a feeling that she couldn't shake.

She rubbed her head. "What is going on around here?" she asked herself aloud.

Tommy stood next to her and solemnly looked up at her. "Maybe we should try to find Dad."

"Maybe," she said.

"Brett told me what happened there."

"At the school?"

"Yeah. He said the janitor got set on fire."

"*What?*"

Tommy just nodded.

Carmen racked her brain. She didn't trust Brett as far as she could throw him, but her dad had gone to the school for something, and nothing had been in the news yet. If it was true, then it was just another item to add to the long list of bizarre occurrences that had been happening lately; odd sensations that she couldn't explain, a missing child, bizarre symbols, and now a man being immolated? A pang of fear tapped on each disc of her spine, climbing from her lower back up to the base of her neck. The words of Peter, the man in the jail cell, echoed in her head and she shivered. Maybe the witch was real...

She turned to her brother. "Yeah, I think it's time we went to the school."

— CHAPTER TEN —

CLUES IN THE DARK

They crossed a row of tall trees and the school came into view. When they saw that the parking lot was empty and there were no flashing lights, their hearts sank.

"They're already gone..." Tommy said.

"Maybe Brett was lying," Carmen suggested.

Tommy squinted through the darkness, spotting something. "No, look!" He pointed his finger toward the front of the school in the distance. Carmen strained to see it, but Tommy took off running.

"Hey, slow down!" The night was bitterly cold and Carmen already had a bad feeling about this.

When they crossed the parking lot, the truth came into focus for them. Yellow police tape stretched across the entrance like a spider web.

"So they *were* here," Tommy said. He reached into his coat pocket and pulled out a magnifying glass, dragging it along the tape and inspecting it with a keen eye.

"Why on Earth do you have a magnifying glass?" Carmen asked with a smirk.

He turned to her as if she had just asked the most foolish question. "Every good adventurer should have a magnifying glass." Carmen shrugged, and Tommy started to duck under the tape.

"Hey!" she shouted, grabbing him by the collar and pulling him back.

Tommy stumbled and then righted himself. "What was that about?" he asked.

"You're not going in there. Are you crazy? We came here to see Dad, not go skulking around a dark school... a *crime scene*."

"Well, Dad's not here," he said. "But... we are. Shouldn't we at least take a look?"

"No!"

"But didn't you say you wanted to know what's going on?" he argued. "I mean, don't you want to know what the witch is doing and try to stop her before she hurts more people?"

Carmen grimaced. Sometimes she really hated her little brother, but it was a hate that came out of love, a paradoxical concept that made sense only to her. She looked around at the dark schoolyard and the empty street. There was no one in sight, and the night seemed peaceful aside from the bone-rattling cold chill that swept through them. She turned back to the police tape and stared at the dark entrance to the school behind it.

Carmen pulled out her phone and looked at the time. "Five minutes," she said to her brother. "After five minutes, I'm pulling you out of there and we're leaving, no ifs, ands, or buts."

Tommy nodded. "Deal."

Carmen carefully climbed through the police tape without tearing it. "Oh, I can't believe I'm doing this."

When she was through to the other side, she gingerly pulled the tape apart just a little so that Tommy would have an easier time getting through. When they were on the other side, both of their hearts beat madly. They felt like rebels—Carmen like a criminal, and Tommy like a treasure hunter. Slowly, they both turned and faced the darkened mouth of the school.

"I don't suppose you have a flashlight, do you?" Carmen asked.

Tommy's eyes went wide and he shook his head. "Crap, I didn't think of that." He slid his magnifying glass back into his coat, making a mental note to carry a flashlight on him as well from now on.

They cautiously stepped into the school, and when the door slammed behind them, they both jumped.

Carmen unlocked her phone and used it for light to see in the darkness. The blackness was overwhelming and smothering, like a thick paste was swimming through the air, making each breath harder than the last. To Carmen it had already felt like five minutes, though they had just stepped in.

"Let's make this quick," she said. "Where did this guy die?"

"Near the furnace," Tommy replied.

"Where's the furnace?"

"In the basement, I think."

"Of course it is," she muttered. "Do you know how to get there?"

Tommy thought for a minute, his face tilting up and his eyes looking through the darkness wistfully, as if he didn't have a care in the world. "Hmm, I think it's that way." He pointed through the dark.

They followed the hall in that direction, turning a corner and seeing another long stretch. They were both taken aback by how quiet it was in here and unnerved by how they could hear each of their own footsteps clapping in their ears like a pair of hands right next to them.

"I still want a Halloween costume," Tommy said, still upset that they had to ditch his Spider-Man costume in the panic of the grocery store.

Carmen rolled her eyes. "Not this again. We'll get you something; stop worrying about it. In case you haven't noticed, we're a little busy right now."

"A good adventurer always keeps his eye open for opportunity," he replied as he marched through the darkness.

She nudged him in the ribs. "What would I do without you?" She smiled and continued down the hallway with him.

Tommy carefully searched each door and room, trying to remember where he would occasionally see the janitor disappear.

"Right there!" he exclaimed, pointing.

Carmen looked at the door ahead carefully. "Are you sure? Because I don't want to be getting lost in here."

He thought for a moment, then he nodded.

"Okay..." she said. Severe apprehension expanded in her chest like a balloon, and she felt herself get lightheaded. She reached out and wrapped her fingers around the cold metal of the handle, then she slowly pulled it open, like if she took any action too quickly, the evil lurking in the darkness would be roused and come after them. When they were through the door, she found a light switch and flicked it, but nothing happened. She made a disapproving noise then looked at her brother. "Hold my hand."

He grabbed it, and she carefully led him down the stairs, making sure he didn't tumble and hurt himself. The air became colder once they reached the basement, almost feeling like they were outside again. Carmen couldn't understand why that was, and her teeth chattered. She looked at her phone. "Has it been five minutes yet?" she muttered to herself.

"Look at that!" Tommy said.

Carmen moved the light from the phone ahead of them and they saw black marks of some sort painted on the floor. They crept forward and took a closer look, Carmen glancing around each corner as they went, expecting something to jump out at them. Upon closer inspection, the black marks appeared to be scorching and soot.

She pressed her hand to her mouth. "Oh my God. This is where it happened. But Dad must have moved the, uh... body."

"Hmm," Tommy said, pulling his magnifying glass out again. "Let's take a look over here."

"Yes, Chief Inspector," Carmen said sarcastically.

They rounded a corner and found a small room. The smell was terrible, like the whole building had been used as a barbecue. Carmen pinched her nose. "That is awful," she said.

But Tommy didn't seem perturbed. The light shone on the furnace ahead, and he approached it.

"Don't get too close," Carmen warned. She stepped into the room to meet him, and held a hand on his shoulder to make sure he didn't stray.

The mouth of the furnace was horribly warped, and the door was missing. The fire inside was out, and heavy black scorch marks and soot were everywhere. Carmen moved the light up the wall, seeing the extent of the damage, then she passed it over something strange and stopped.

Tommy immediately walked up to the wall and stretched up on his toes, holding the magnifying glass to his eye.

"What do we have here?" he asked inquisitively.

"Is that... another symbol?" Carmen asked, seeing the scorched heart with a dagger through it plastered on the wall.

"It's from the witch," Tommy concluded.

"What does it mean?"

Tommy racked his brain. "There was a rope on the tree where Jeremy disappeared, there was an antenna thingy in the town square under the pumpkins, and now there's a heart by the furnace..." He thought for a long moment, but he couldn't come up with an answer.

"And what's this?" Carmen asked, bending down low and turning the light to the floor. Just inside the doorway, there was a strand of timothy-grass. "Dad must've missed this," she said.

Tommy bent and inspected it. He picked it up and twisted it in his hand. "It's not burned," he remarked. He looked around. "If there was a big fire here, this would be burnt to a crisp, but it looks like it was just picked."

Carmen narrowed her eyes. "Where have I seen this stuff before?" In fact, there was only one place she had ever seen it, only one part of town where this grew, but at the moment, she couldn't place it. Tommy was similarly stumped, then Carmen looked at her phone and saw that their five minutes had passed. "Okay, time's up," she said, feeling the heaviness on her heart alleviate a little. "Let's get out of here."

Tommy didn't want to leave yet, but he knew better than to cross his big sister. He snatched up the strand of timothy-grass and carefully slid it into a pocket in his coat.

They left the school quickly the way they had come and slipped through the police tape. Their hearts settled down almost immediately, but their brains still raced, trying to understand what it all meant.

— CHAPTER ELEVEN —

MENAGERIE

When the two of them headed home, it was just past nine o'clock. They walked through the town streets hardly saying a word to each other, each of them too busy thinking about what had gone on lately, and it took quite a few blocks before Carmen stopped, noticing how peculiar everything was.

"Does something seem strange to you?" she asked her brother.

Tommy looked around. "Like what?"

"Well, where is everyone, for one?" She checked her phone and saw that though it was late, there still should have been a little bit of activity in the town. But ever since they'd left the school, they hadn't seen a single soul. It was like they had stepped through a portal when they left the school and been transported into a ghost town. "Like, where are the search parties looking for that boy?"

They both stayed silent and listened, trying to hear the call of the boy's name. They glanced around, but they saw no flashlights anywhere, no patrolling police cars, *nothing*.

"I don't know," Tommy said. But now he fully realized the oddness of the situation.

The only sound that could be heard was the gentle wind rolling across the town in waves, lingering in tree leaves before flitting off into the darkness.

They both gulped at the same time, and they carried on silently, each of them suddenly aware of how alone they felt. The streetlights glowed dimly in the dark, and they didn't provide them much solace from their feelings of uneasiness.

As they continued their trek home, a stray cat walked out from behind a building up ahead. It crossed the street to their side and stopped on the sidewalk in front of them.

Carmen and Tommy lurched to a stop.

The cat turned and looked at them, then it arched its back and hissed at them.

Carmen waited, finding the situation strange, but assuming that the cat would move on. But it didn't. In fact, it started walking toward them, slinking one paw at a time, closer and closer and never taking its eyes off them. It hissed again.

"What's it doing?" Tommy asked, frightened.

"I don't know." She grabbed her brother's hand and pulled him onto the road. They quickly skirted around the cat and continued along the sidewalk, increasing their pace. She looked over her shoulder and saw that the cat had turned and was still slinking toward them. But it was moving a lot more slowly than they were, and she breathed a sigh of relief as she looked forward again.

More cats came out of the woodwork ahead, most of them stray and mangy. They came from all directions around them and slowly closed in, all of them staring and hissing.

"What's going on?" Tommy asked.

"I don't know!" Carmen repeated. She gripped her brother's hand tighter and they broke into a run. The cats followed slowly, only slinking after them, and somehow that made it even scarier. Their path was choked out ahead by more felines, and now there were about three dozen of them getting closer. Carmen stopped and looked around, seeing a house up ahead on their left whose entire yard was fenced in with short chain-link. "Over here!" she cried, pulling her brother to the gate. She opened it and ushered Tommy into the front yard, then she spun and clasped the gate shut.

They backed away as the cats clustered on the other side, but the felines didn't try to jump over or get through; they just stopped and sat up, their tails seductively gliding from side to side.

The bitter cold nipped at Carmen and Tommy and made them shiver, and they turned away from the gate as a sea of glowing eyes watched.

"We've got to get out of here," Carmen said. The property was dark, and it seemed like no one was home. They traipsed around the side of the house to the backyard and spotted a short stack of old truck tires sitting next to a shed and the tall wooden fence closing them in.

"I think we can get out there," she said. "Do you think you can get over it?"

He looked up at the fence like a challenge. "A good adventurer—"

"Yeah, yeah," she said, cutting him off. A wave suddenly washed over her and she stumbled, feeling light-headed.

"What is it?" Tommy asked, concerned.

"I don't know," she replied. "My heart's still beating like crazy from those cats, and suddenly I don't feel so well. It's hard to describe. I just don't feel right." She let the feeling roll through her and pass, then she took a moment to compose herself.

A dog house sat next to them that neither of them had noticed, and a pair of glowing eyes appeared as the canine's head rose.

A loud, sharp bark pierced the night and made the two of them jump.

Carmen and Tommy looked over their shoulders and saw the flash of eyes for only a second before the dog lunged out of the house and attacked them. A chain was attached to its collar, and it stretched out and snapped taut just as the dog's teeth chomped at Carmen's neck, narrowly missing it. She fell to the ground and scrambled across the cold grass, pressing herself against the fence.

The dog kept at the end of his leash, fighting against it and jumping and gnashing his teeth madly. Carmen and Tommy only had about a foot and a half of free space between the fence and the dog, and they tried to sidle over to the tires as quickly as possible.

But they could hear the wood in the doghouse that the other end of the chain was attached to starting to warp and crack from the force of the mutt.

"Get up here!" Carmen shouted frantically as she ushered her brother onto the tires. The stack was wobbly with someone standing on it, but she braced him. Reaching up, she helped give him a boost as he jumped up and grabbed the top of the fence, slowly pulling himself over. He swung his legs over the top then fell to the other side and disappeared from view.

She could feel the dog's hot breath on her ankles as it jumped and snapped its teeth behind her. She scrambled onto the tire stack, and she felt it wobble severely under her weight. It felt like if she made any sudden movements, the stack would slide out from under her.

The dog lunged again and the wood broke apart, freeing it from its tether.

Carmen's heart seized and she made a panicked jump for the fence. The tire directly under her feet slid off the stack and she lost her footing, only getting a halfhearted jump. She stretched her arms out in desperation and hooked them over top of the fence, but the rest of her body was hanging limply against the face of it.

The dog lunged forward and snapped at her ankle, catching her by the cuff of her jeans. She screamed and Tommy yelled from the other side, asking if she was okay. He jumped up and tried to help her, but he couldn't even reach her arms.

Carmen pulled with all of her might to get up and fight against the dog, kicking her leg and trying to get free. Her body slowly rose, a feat that she would normally not have the strength for, but she did now in her desperation just like a mother suddenly gaining the strength to lift a car off her baby. The dog yanked its head one way and pulled her back, and she swung her leg out in a wide kick and pulled the dog the other way, finally breaking its grip on her pant leg.

The dog staggered to the side and took a moment to regain itself before attacking again, but that gave Carmen all the time she needed to get herself over the fence and tumble over into the next yard.

Tommy rushed to her and made sure she wasn't badly injured.

Carmen wheezed and struggled to get up onto her rubbery legs. As they composed themselves and searched for an exit, they saw two St. Bernards sitting on the back deck of the new yard they were in. When the dogs spotted them, they slowly raised up onto their haunches, their eyes glowing like marbles.

"You gotta be kidding me," Carmen said.

In the next moment, they both fled in a panic while the large dogs barked and chased them.

There was a low hedge closing off the backyard in front of them, and Carmen and Tommy dove for it. They landed on the top and got tangled in the dense branches that swam under their weight. They flopped like fishes, then they toppled over onto grass on the other side and found themselves on an empty street.

They got to their feet and ran the rest of the way home. The town was still empty, and Carmen began to wonder if this was some kind of strange nightmare she was having. But the pain in her legs and the biting cold of the wind told her it wasn't. They ran from street to street on autopilot, and they soon found themselves on a familiar route. Carmen looked up in a tree next to them and saw the familiar owl sitting on a branch and tracking their movement. Then her heart sank as it stretched its wings and sailed off its perch. She let out a pained cry, the fear overwhelming her now.

The owl squawked in the night somewhere behind them, and she felt a gush of wind across her neck and a hard slap of feathers smacked her in the back of the head. Its beak snapped at her neck and sliced it.

Carmen clamped a hand to it then held it in front of her face, seeing a drop of blood under the pale glow of the streetlights.

The owl circled around in the sky and dove for them again.

"It's coming back!" Tommy cried, looking over his shoulder.

They both ducked as they ran, and this time the owl swooped for Tommy, flapping at his ear, but missing its bite.

The rest of their path was a blur, but then Carmen looked up, every cell in her body desperate for an oasis of solitude and protection, and she spotted just that.

"Our house!" she yelled, pointing ahead.

They pumped their legs as hard as they could, but their muscles were tired. The owl circled around and made another diving attack, but they both anticipated it and split up from each other as it swooped through the middle of them. They watched it glide by in front of them and climb up into the sky. But this time it didn't come back. It flew up and up, seemingly losing itself in the stars, and then it made a wide curve and flew out of sight.

Carmen and Tommy doubled over, placing their hands on their knees and panting for the oxygen they'd lost. They glanced up at each other weakly, their looks saying more than any words could. Then Carmen's eyes widened.

"What?" he asked.

"Tommy..." She looked over his shoulder, and he slowly turned.

Down at the end of the street, just behind the illumination of the last streetlight, a figure stood in the middle of it. It was hard to see in the shadows, but it looked humanoid. No features were visible, as if the entire figure were shrouded in black robes. Carmen squinted her eyes, trying to discern what it was as her gaze traced the vague shape of it. The figure was short and wide, and the top of it tapered up to a point. It almost looked like a big black hat.

The figure glided like a wraith along the street, and just as it was about to reach the edge of the streetlight's glow, the bulb went out, casting that whole section in darkness. The wraith moved through and the next streetlight went out ahead of it. Carmen and Tommy watched, paralyzed by their fear.

Carmen opened her mouth, trying to say something, but she couldn't get the words out. She summoned enough courage to move her arm and grab for her brother's. When she found it, she tugged him toward the house as the strange apparition closed in on them. They moved sluggishly, but they made their way up to the porch, finally managing to break their gazes with the figure. Carmen fumbled in her pocket for her house key, then struggled to slide it into the lock. When it was in, she turned it and opened the door, shoving her brother inside and glancing over her shoulder.

The figure crossed the sidewalk to the row of hedges lining the front of the property. And then it glided through it.

Carmen yelped and slammed the door behind her, locking it. She ran through the dark house with her brother, fleeing down the hall and stopping at the end of it, looking around at the bedrooms and wondering where to hide, what to do.

"Are we safe?" Tommy asked frantically.

"I don't know!" Carmen said.

"Can it come through the door?"

"I don't know!" She suddenly remembered the necklace that Peter had told her to take from his effects when he was arrested, and while it was only useless junk to her before, now it was like a crucifix to a priest battling a demon. She ran into her bedroom and ripped open her drawer where she'd put it. When she saw it, she let out a breath of relief, snatching it up in her hands.

There was a scratching sound at the front door.

"Come in my room!" Tommy said. "We can hide there!" He pulled his sister into his bedroom and dragged her around the bed to his makeshift cubbyhole between his bed and the wall. They both sank down onto their bellies, twisting around and climbing in feet-first. It was a tight squeeze with the two of them, but they hunkered in as far as possible, lowering their chins to the carpet and waiting as Carmen clutched the necklace in her hand.

They waited and listened in the darkness.

The lock on the front door slowly twisted open.

Their skin crawled at the sound.

Then the door was slowly pushed open and the creak of its hinges echoed through the house. A heavy foot came down on the floor, then another. There was a long pause of silence, and then the footsteps continued through the house, rounding the corner and coming down the hallway.

Carmen and Tommy clutched each other tightly, peering out from the cubbyhole at the doorway to Tommy's bedroom in sheer terror.

Then the footsteps entered Tommy's room.

Carmen clapped a hand around her brother's mouth so he wouldn't scream.

"What are you two doing?" their father said. His tall figure stood in the doorway, silhouetted by the nightlight plugged into an outlet in the hallway behind him.

"N-Nothing," Carmen stuttered. "We're, uh, just playing."

Robert paused. "All right then," he said. There was a slowness to his voice that was unnatural, like each word was said very distinctly and carefully, like all the warmness that used to be in it had been stripped away.

"Dad?" Carmen said.

"Yes, Sweetpea?"

"Why are you holding your gun?"

The silhouette tilted its head down and looked at the firearm clutched in its hand. It slowly drew its arm back and returned the gun to its holster.

"Sorry about that, Sweetpea," he said. Then he turned and walked out of the room, heading to the other end of the house.

Carmen looked at her brother and saw his eyes widened in terror. They were illuminated in a dim rose-colored glow, and Carmen looked down to see the stone attached to the necklace clutched in her hand was glowing.

They stayed in the cubby for a long time, eventually hearing their father turn on lights and going about his normal business in the house, almost as if nothing strange happened at all.

Carmen looked at her brother. "First thing tomorrow morning, we're finding this Peter fellow and asking him some questions."

"Yeah," Tommy said, never agreeing with his sister more than he did now.

— CHAPTER TWELVE —

Sit-Down

Morning broke and the sun arced up over the land as a thin fog rolled across the town. Carmen and Tommy both woke up in their own beds, stretching and yawning after a good night's sleep. They both separately experienced the same sensation of feeling like the events of the night before were just a crazy dream. They got up and got dressed, going to the kitchen for breakfast.

Carmen looked out the living room window and saw that the cruiser was gone. Their father must have already been at the station. She went into the kitchen and poured herself a glass of orange juice as Tommy came in behind her, rubbing his eyes. She turned and looked at him carefully. "How did you sleep?"

"Pretty good," he replied. He lazily dragged his feet across the tile floor and took the glass of orange juice that she offered him. He walked around the couch and plunked down on it, turning on the TV and watching cartoons in his pajamas.

Carmen watched the back of his head. It truly did seem like he wasn't fazed by all this stuff, or at least he hid it well. She couldn't say the same thing for herself, and though the brightness of the morning had washed away all the fears of the night before, she still felt worked up and wanted to put an end to all of this.

"Why don't I make us some breakfast?" she said.

Tommy turned around and kneeled on the couch. "And then we'll go see Peter, right?"

"I'm glad you still want to," she said.

She made them French toast just the way he liked it, then they sat and ate in silence. When they were done, they got dressed and cleaned up, then they put on their coats and boots.

The town was nothing like the way it was the night before. First of all, there were cars driving by, people walking around, and birds peacefully fluttering through the air, and nothing seemed out of the ordinary.

"Where do we find him?" Tommy asked.

"Police station," Carmen replied. "It's the only way we'll be able to."

"I thought he said they were going to let him go."

"Yeah, but they would still have a record of his address."

"Ah," Tommy said, his face lighting up. "You'd make a good detective."

"I'm thrilled."

They waited on the corner for the bus and it stopped and picked them up. Carmen tried saying hi to the driver, but just like before, he was cold; hostile, even.

A few sets of eyes moved over them as they made their way to an open set of seats. That same look of irritation they'd seen in the townspeople before was still there, but now it seemed to slide more toward apathy. Most of them had blank stares on their faces, though a few seemed grouchy.

They hopped off on Carson Street and walked the rest of the way to the station. When they got inside, they saw a calm scene. An officer was working behind the front desk, and they saw a few others milling around through the hallway.

"Can I help you?" the officer behind the desk asked them sternly.

Carmen and Tommy were taken aback, knowing Officer Brown pretty well for a few years now.

"Just going to see our Dad," Carmen said.

The officer grumbled something under his breath, then he turned back to his paperwork.

Tommy cocked a strange eye at the man, then they went to their father's office. It was empty. A hand fell on Tommy's shoulder suddenly and he spun around.

Don stood there, smiling. "Looking for your dad?"

"Uh, yeah," Carmen said.

He turned his head toward the entrance and narrowed his eyes. "He's out right now. Don't know when he'll be back."

"Do you know where he went?"

Don's face suddenly scrunched up, like he was trying to hold back a sneeze. He wiped his hand across his face, then he let out a long yawn. This was cut short by his nose and eyebrows scrunching up as if he were angry. Then he settled. "Can't say, can't say." He turned and wandered down the hallway, and the kids were left bewildered, watching him go.

"Come on," Carmen whispered to her brother.

"What's wrong with them?" Tommy asked.

"Let's not worry about that now. We need to find out where Peter lives."

They passed all the offices, some of the officers giving them a suspicious eye, and some of them ignoring them completely. They rounded the corner and came to the booking desk just before the jail cells. There was an officer sitting behind the desk, reading a book.

He pulled down his glasses and looked at them. "You two shouldn't be back here." He rubbed his nose and adjusted his glasses on his round face, then he stroked his mustache and rested his hand on his rotund belly.

Tommy looked up at him with apologetic eyes. "We were just, we were... we were playing back here before and I lost my ball in one of the cells at the back there."

The officer closed his book and leaned forward, his desk digging into his gut. He twisted his head and peered down the stretch of jail cells.

"Can you get it back for me?"

"For you, Tommy? Anything." The officer stood up with a smile, then he forcefully shoved his chair away from him and it skittered along the floor and slammed into the wall with a bang.

Carmen and Tommy backed up, surprised, and they waited on pins and needles as the officer calmly walked down to the other end of the cells.

"*Okay, now!*" Carmen whispered. They worked their way around the desk and skimmed through the booking ledger. They didn't see the name on the open set of pages, so Carmen flipped the page, then she ran her finger down each line until she found the name 'Peter'.

"Here it is," she whispered. "Peter Simpson... 86 Somerset Drive."

"I don't see any ball back here!" the officer announced, anger rising in his voice. He turned around, ready to pick a bone with the kids, but they were gone. He waddled back around his desk and pulled his chair to him, sinking into it and peacefully opening his book as he adjusted his glasses on his nose.

Out in the lobby, Carmen and Tommy headed for the doors, Don giving them a friendly smile on the way by his office. But before they reached the exit, Carmen stopped and looked up at the TV set hanging in the corner. It was tuned to the news, and the familiar reporter was on the air.

"Yes, just this morning we can report that two children have disappeared, Penny Carpenter and Joey Kurtz. Both vanished from their homes and are now considered missing by the police." The reporter looked at the cameraman and said something that didn't seem appropriate on air, then she looked into the camera and said, "So anyway, that's the news, I guess..." She dropped the microphone and walked off into the distance.

Two more kids missing. Carmen looked around the police station, but there was no hustle and bustle among any of the officers. In fact, if anything, they should have been out searching for them. And there were no crowds outside demanding answers like there were before.

"It's like nobody cares anymore," Carmen said.

"What do you mean?" Tommy asked.

"I think I see what's going on here. It's like Peter said... the adults are being distracted while the kids are taken one by one."

— — —

Carmen knocked on the door.

There was silence for a long time, then finally they both heard someone shuffling around inside. The footsteps came up to the door then stopped.

They looked up and noticed a peephole in the door, and they saw a shadow moving behind it. A chain was slid inside, then the door opened a crack. "Yes?" the man asked.

"Peter?" Carmen asked cautiously. "We met you when you were in, uh... jail."

His eyes lit up, then he opened the door all the way. "Oh, it's you!" He stepped out onto the porch and looked around, then he urged them inside.

Tommy looked up at his sister, wordlessly asking if it was okay, knowing that he wasn't supposed to go in the homes or vehicles of strangers.

But Carmen patted him on the back and nodded, and they both went inside. Peter closed the door behind them.

"Come in, please," he said. "Make yourself at home. The living room's just over there."

Carmen and Tommy walked down the hallway that left something to be desired in the cleanliness department, then they came into his living room, a hodgepodge of mild semblance, yet also mess and strange decorations. Bizarre art hung on his walls, and he had a big dream catcher hanging up in the corner of the room. Peculiar necklaces and other small jewelry and artifacts were hanging around from the walls and sitting on tables, similar to the necklace he had given her. A pungent odor hung in the air, like old incense. Carmen looked at the only couch she saw, which was half-covered in musty blankets.

"Oh, pardon me," he said, rushing into the room. "I didn't expect to have company." He cleaned the blankets off the couch for them.

"Oh, don't worry about it," Carmen said, already feeling uncomfortable. Tommy marched ahead and sat down at the end, and Carmen sat in the middle.

"Tea? Coffee?" Peter asked.

"No thanks," Carmen replied. "We're actually here to talk to you about the... well, I guess there's nothing else to call it but a witch."

The look on Peter's face suddenly became grave. He sat down on the couch next to them and clasped his hands under his chin. His voice got low, almost to a whisper, and he said, "You've seen her, haven't you?"

Carmen and Tommy both looked at each other uneasily, then they swiveled their heads to Peter and nodded. "We think we saw her last night out in the street," Tommy said. "She chased us to our house. She was like a... like a..."

"A ghost," Carmen said.

"I see," Peter replied, disturbed by this information.

Tommy reached into his coat pocket and pulled out the strand of timothy-grass they'd taken from the school. "We found this where the janitor was killed," Tommy said.

Peter took it from him, his brow furrowed in confusion. "I didn't hear about that," he said. "They didn't report it on the news, at least."

"That's one of the things we've been wondering about," Carmen added. "Everybody's been acting really strange around here, including our dad. We can't figure out what's going on."

Peter put the timothy-grass down on his lap. "Did you both hear about the event three years ago?"

"Yeah, mostly from our dad. We also saw some stuff on the news, and heard things from other kids, but I don't know what was true or not. They kept saying that a witch lived at Halloween House. Well, where she used to live, anyway."

"I was there that night," Peter said. "I watched the house burn."

Carmen's eyes widened. "Was that..."

Peter shook his head. "I didn't set the fire. A part of me was glad that it happened, but at the time I feared that something far worse would occur because of it. It turns out I was right."

"So what's happening around here?"

Peter leaned back. "The witch has cast a number of spells over the town. Have you seen the strange symbols popping up everywhere? The lasso? The broadcast tower?"

They both nodded.

"I just saw on the news this morning that two more children were taken." Peter shook his head. "But it's going to get a lot worse, I fear. And at the sites of their disappearances, they found two more lasso symbols."

Carmen leaned forward. "I didn't hear about those. So what are they?"

"They're sigils. They're shapes that, while seemingly meaningless on their own, are charged to have a certain meaning. It's clear that the lasso means ensnarement."

"What's that?" Tommy asked.

"That symbol only shows up when children are taken," Peter explained. "Each time the witch does it, her ability to do it again grows. Each kidnapping charges the sigil's power and manipulates circumstances to more easily take place in the future."

Carmen's head was spinning. "And the broadcast tower?" As soon as she'd said it, she finally realized the answer.

"Notice that it's in the town square?" Peter asked. "As in, the very center of town?"

Carmen nodded. "That's what's making everyone act funny," she said. "But why does it seem to affect the adults mostly? And why mostly at night? In the daytime it's not as bad."

"Everyone's thoughts are unprotected, but I keep mine well-guarded," he said, looking around at all his charms and items.

"What does that mean?" she asked.

"A spell can be cast by any means and for any purpose, but it seems clear to me that the spell that the witch cast over the town feeds on their fear. When the children started going missing, the town's fear grew, and the more it grows, the more influenced they are by the spell. That's why things get worse at night; in the daytime things don't seem as bad, but at night people start to grow fearful of their own shadow, especially adults." He looked at Tommy. "Kids seem to be more fearless, for some reason. Most adults are walking through this world terrified on a good day. That's why you don't seem to be too affected by it either, young miss; you haven't experienced the joy of paying taxes yet, I'm assuming."

She chuckled. "It's Carmen, by the way."

Peter extended his hand and she shook it.

"So what do we do? How do we fix all this?" she asked.

Peter sat deep in thought for a long moment. "I'm not sure you two should be doing anything. You're still too young. I'm afraid the witch will go after you."

Tommy gulped.

"I see on the news also that each missing child seems to have a gingerbread cookie found where they were last seen. A cookie seems to be the mark of the witch, so to speak. If you see one, your time may be short."

"We have to do something," Carmen said exasperatedly. "It doesn't seem like anyone else can help, not even my father, and he's the chief of police, for crying out loud."

"Your father's the chief?" he asked.

She nodded.

"Hmm... Well those children have to be found. I fear what she's going to do with them come Halloween night. I hope it's not too late already."

"But how do we find them? How do we even know where she is?"

He picked up the timothy-grass and inspected it. "You said you found this at the site of someone's death?"

Tommy nodded. "Yeah, it was sitting next to the furnace, but it wasn't burned. And there was another symbol on the wall."

"Tell me."

"It was like a heart with a knife through it," Tommy said.

Peter shook his head. "I haven't seen that one before. It could have something to do with draining the lifeblood—killing, obviously." He paused. "So the victim wasn't a child, but this grass's presence still seems too strange to be unimportant."

"What about the house?" Carmen asked. "Halloween House?"

Peter considered this, but he shook his head. "I found the courage to go up there once after the incident, but it's just a burned-out husk. Nothing left, really. I'm not convinced anymore that she's tied to a location, but the children are." He twisted the timothy-grass in his fingers. "Perhaps wherever this originated from is where they are being kept."

"Do you know where it grows?" Carmen asked. "I've been trying to figure out where I remember seeing it, but I'm drawing a blank."

"Sorry," he said. "I'm not sure."

"How do you know so much about the witch, mister?" Tommy asked.

As Peter considered him, they both saw the age and wear in his eyes and on his face. It told half of the story by itself. "I was a boy not much older than you when I first ran into her," he explained. "I was playing with some friends out in the woods and I got separated from them. I saw her house at the top of the hill, though we never called it Halloween House back then. All we knew was that an old, crazy woman lived there. Hardly anyone ever saw her even back then, but she was still just as old and haggard as she was three years ago, like she doesn't age."

Tommy gulped again.

A squirrel rummaged around the yard outside Peter's living room window, then it climbed up to the windowsill, peering through the glass at the three of them as they talked. None of them noticed the small animal, but it sat and watched, its eyes unblinking.

"I was scared, but curious," he continued. "So I went up to the house. There was a homeless boy that used to live in this town that was my age. I saw him often, and he would always wander around and beg for money. Then a little bit before that time, he disappeared and no one ever saw him again. And because he was homeless, no one really batted an eye or looked for him. One day he asked me what time it was while he sat on a street corner and begged, and I felt so bad for him that I gave him the very watch off my wrist. So when I climbed up the hill that day and found the watch I'd given him half-buried in the mud not far from the house, I had a sinking feeling that I knew what happened to him.

"The darkness was just starting to set in, and I crept up to the house quietly so I wouldn't be seen or heard. There was a light on in the basement, and I snuck up to the window and peered inside. I saw a pair of shoes sitting on a messy table, with a pile of clothes next to it. I recognized those clothes and those shoes, because I saw them on the boy every day. I leaned closer to the window to get a better look, and I saw a foot lying on a table. I couldn't see the rest of his body from my angle, but in trying to do so, my head bumped into the glass.

"The witch jumped into view in the basement, and I saw her face clearly. I'll never forget that image. The next thing I know, I'm running away through the woods, and I hear the door of her house open behind me and her crazed, incessant cries. She chased me, and she wouldn't stop. I got tired, but she kept going. She eventually caught up to me and tripped me, grabbing onto my leg and dragging me back toward her house. But I managed to kick her and knock her down. I looked around for the biggest stick I could find, and when I found one, I hit her in the head with it. She fell over, and I ran. I never stopped, but I kept checking over my shoulder to see if she was coming after me. Just before she was out of view, I saw her rise, but I was far enough away. After that, I never went near that house again until after she was killed. I tried telling everyone what happened to me and the other boy at the time, but no one believed me. Everyone started treating me like I was crazy. And throughout all the years since then, I've done a lot of research on witches, because I saw a big black cauldron sitting in her basement, and I couldn't figure out what it was for."

Carmen and Tommy were both on the edge of the couch, their eyes wide.

"So she really *is* a witch," Tommy muttered.

"But it looks like she didn't really die," Peter added.

"How do we stop her?" Carmen asked, a steely determination in her eyes.

Peter sighed. "I don't know," he admitted. "Everything I know about dealing with witches are with ones that are still alive. How do you kill something that's already dead?"

"Well you must know something after all these years!" Carmen cried.

"I'll look into it," he said. "Can you kids meet me tomorrow morning at the school?"

"But that's already Halloween," Carmen protested. "We don't have much time."

"I know," he said. "But I'm going to need some time to study. In the meantime, do you still have that witch mirror I told you about?"

"Witch mirror?" Carmen said, confused. "What's that?" She reached into her pocket and pulled up the necklace with the rose-colored stone that had glowed the night before and was now back to its normal appearance. "You mean this?"

He nodded. "It's called a witch mirror," he reiterated. "It's magically charged to repel spells that the witch casts. It's not a cure-all for everything she does, but it will help protect you. Make sure you keep it with you and your brother at all times." Peter stood up and walked to the living room window, looking around suspiciously.

The squirrel jumped down from the windowsill and darted off into a bush.

Peter turned back to the two of them. "Remember, tomorrow at the school, as early as you can come. I'll be there."

Carmen and Tommy nodded and thanked him, then they left.

— — —

After they were gone, Peter puttered around his kitchen, fixing himself some tea. A car went by outside the window, but he wasn't paying attention. His mind was racing about all the information he told the kids, and he tried to figure out how to stop what was going on.

A car door slammed shut outside.

Peter perked up, hearing footsteps approaching his door. Then a knock came. He set down his tea and quietly walked around to the front door, peering through the peephole. He saw two police officers standing on his porch. He held his breath and waited, unsure of what to do.

"Open up, sir, we know you're in there," one of them said.

Peter sighed, then he opened the door. "Good afternoon, officers. What can I help you with?"

"Would you turn around and put your hands behind your back, please?" Don said.

"What's this about?" Peter asked.

Don grabbed him and forcefully turned him around as his partner pulled out handcuffs and slapped them on his wrists.

"What am I being charged with?"

"You have the right to remain silent..." Don started as they carried him off to the cruiser and carted him off to jail.

— CHAPTER THIRTEEN —

BACK-ALLEY SPAT

Carmen and Tommy walked down the street, heading past the town square downtown. They glanced over at it, and each felt a chill roll up their spine. They couldn't feel any effects from the sigil, but now that they were armed with the information that it fed off of their fear, they tried to stay in control of their thoughts and take a calmer approach and attitude to everything.

Townspeople walked around them on the foggy day, slipping in and out of stores. Cars rolled by slowly and unevenly. A black Ford pickup truck rolled forward and veered out of its lane too much, and the front bumper crunched into a parked car on the side of the street.

Carmen and Tommy looked at it wide-eyed as the driver backed up, then casually drove off as if nothing happened.

"So what should we do between now and tomorrow when we meet Peter at the school?" Tommy asked.

Carmen considered this for a moment. "Hmm, I don't know. I do know that we should keep our outings to the daytime only. And at night, we'll stay inside and use the witch mirror."

Tommy nodded.

"Even if we can't stop the witch by tomorrow night," Carmen said, "hopefully it will all blow over after that."

"But what about the kids that've been taken?"

A heaviness was pinned to her heart at the words, and her lip trembled in sadness.

They carried on down the street, distracted, as a silver sedan sped by in front of them and smashed into a telephone pole. The driver was thrown out the windshield and crumpled into the pole himself, his limp body coming to rest on the mangled hood of the car.

Carmen and Tommy yelped and they both backed up, bumping into the wall of a store. They stared at the scene in horror and then slowly looked around to find everyone else going about their business as normal. A few passersby glanced at the accident, but most ignored it completely like they didn't even see it.

The two of them were speechless as they stood rooted on the spot for what seemed like forever, then Carmen finally pulled Tommy away from the scene. They both walked down the street, feeling numb. Their bodies were shaking, and their blood turned white. They only lasted another block before Tommy told her that he was feeling sick. There was a convenience store next to them, and Carmen told him to go in and use the bathroom. He shuffled through the door, and she waited outside in the cold for him to get back. Her body shook terribly from the horrifying incident she just witnessed, and she tried to keep her own thoughts in check, remembering not to get scared. But if they had gotten to that stretch of road just ten seconds sooner, they may have been badly hurt.

Strange feelings washed over her aside from the shock, and they were those same familiar sensations she'd experienced a couple times on previous nights. She knew now that they were the first symptoms of what everyone else in the town was experiencing. If they had control over them to the degree that she was seeing now, then the townspeople must have really been so far gone to it. She shuddered to think what would become of her if she let herself do the same.

Shouting came from a nearby alley. Carmen took a few strides over to the entrance of it and peeked around the corner.

The narrow alley stretched between stores to the backs of them where all the supplies and garbage were carried in and out. And standing there was Brett, his sister Stacy, and her boyfriend that they'd seen in the car before.

"Vince, stop!" Stacy said.

Vince ignored her. He shoved Brett on the shoulder, easily two or three times his size and age. "I know you took them, you little twerp," he said.

"I didn't take your c-cigarettes," Brett stammered, trying to stand up for himself.

"Like hell," Vince retorted. He wound his arm back and punched Brett in the stomach.

"Brett!" Stacy cried.

He sank down to his knees and fell over on the cold concrete.

"Whatever, I'm out of here," Vince said. "You owe me for those smokes, baby," he said to Stacy as he took another alley out of there.

Stacy looked up at him with hatred, then she turned her attention back to her little brother. "Brett? *Brett!* Are you okay?"

Brett writhed on the ground and moaned, cradling his stomach.

Stacy began crying, and the hot tears streaked down her face and turned the whites of her eyes red. She looked up suddenly and saw Carmen staring at her in surprise. Instead of asking her for help, instead of just simply being embarrassed, Stacy shot up to her feet and came toward her.

"What do you think you're looking at?!" she demanded, marching on the warpath for her.

Carmen took a step back, slowly raising her hands. "I..." It wasn't the reaction she expected.

Now Stacy's face was red with embarrassment that Carmen had witnessed all of that. "What, you think this is *funny?*" she shouted.

"I don't," Carmen said calmly.

But Stacy wouldn't relent. "You think this is a joke?!" She stepped forward and shoved Carmen's chest.

Carmen regained her footing and stood up to Stacy. "Hey! I just saw you guys back there. I didn't mean anything by it!" She wasn't about to back down from Stacy, and she tried her best to remain calm. She felt bad for her and Brett, but Stacy wasn't being very accommodating.

Stacy pushed her again, and in anger, Carmen pushed her back. Despite that, Carmen tried to stay calm. But when Stacy slapped her across the face, all bets were off.

Carmen's hand balled up into a fist as her eyes slowly dragged up to Stacy's face—her target.

"W-What's going on?" Tommy asked, wiping his mouth with the back of his hand.

Stacy and Carmen turned and saw him standing there, looking up at them with bewildered eyes. Now the scene was becoming even more embarrassing for Stacy, but she wouldn't dare hit a child. So she turned her ire on Carmen one last time and spit on her. The ball of saliva sailed through the air and landed on Carmen's neck, then Stacy turned and marched back for Brett.

"Come on, get up," she said, picking him up to his feet and marching him out the other exit as he groaned.

Carmen watched her go, her eyes narrow, as she wiped the spit off with the sleeve of her coat.

— CHAPTER FOURTEEN —

ROAD TRIP

The library was dead silent, with no one in there except for the one woman working at the front. Tommy kept casting suspicious glances over his shoulder down the aisles next to them, like someone would be sneaking up on them at any moment.

Carmen turned the knob of the microfilm reader, looking through old newspapers from throughout the town's history. She had already gone back fifty years, not seeing anything at all about the witch. It seemed that truly no one had ever talked about her when she was living in that house, but what she wanted to know more than anything was just how long she had been living there.

"I'm not finding anything," Carmen said.

Tommy leaned over her shoulder and looked at a newspaper from 1961. "When the clues aren't coming to you, try a new approach," he said. "That's the mark of a go—"

"Good adventurer," Carmen finished, rolling her eyes.

He grabbed the dial from her and twisted it all the way back, going into newspapers from the 1800s.

"I think this is about as far back as you can go," Carmen said. Some of the papers weren't very well-kept, and the print was hard to read on the screen. They both strained their eyes as Carmen took control again and cycled through them.

Their small town seemed a lot smaller back then based off the headlines they were reading, but when they got to a newspaper from 1884, Tommy pointed to the screen.

"What?" Carmen asked.

"Go back, I think I saw something."

She obliged, then she waited for him to point it out.

"There!"

Carmen strained her eyes, as staring at all that type had started to give her a headache, and she saw the headline he was pointing out.

Occult Gypsies from Bulgaria Chased out of Haverford, the headline read.

Carmen read the article carefully. "Oh my God, Tommy, you're a genius!" Tommy smirked. "It says here that a small family immigrated from Bulgaria sometime in the 1870s, and as soon as they arrived, mysterious things started happening in the town." She turned to her brother and smacked him on the shoulder.

"I've heard of Haverford," Tommy said. "That's a few towns over, isn't it?"

"Yeah," Carmen said. "This also says that some of the townsfolk were being... *'mind-controlled'* by the Gypsies until the townspeople chased them out. It says they were exiled and then..." She gulped. "...*burned at the stake*." Carmen turned the dial on the microfilm reader to see the rest of the article. "One got away," she read. "They said she wandered into the woods, taking refuge in them. The townspeople left her alone after that because she kept to herself, but they called her... Look, Tommy, it's right here! They called her the 'Witch of Haverford'." She spun around in her seat and faced him.

Tommy looked up, trying to do the math in his head.

"That means she was over a hundred years old when she died," Carmen said.

"If she was old enough to go into the woods by herself and build a house, then she would've been way older than a hundred," he said.

"How's that possible?"

"Magic?" Tommy suggested.

Carmen smirked and rustled his hair.

"Why does everyone keep doing that?" Tommy asked, fixing it.

Carmen turned back to the microfilm reader and scrolled through more articles, going through them quickly and skimming over the years. But she didn't spot anything else that seemed to relate to the so-called "Witch of Haverford", and if the stories everyone had told her recently were accurate, it seemed like there were probably not many stories to tell because she truly did live in seclusion for the most part, at least secretly. But now that tenuous truce was broken and she was having her revenge.

"Does it say how to stop her?" Tommy asked.

Carmen scoffed. "Yeah, like that would be printed in the newspaper. 'Step one: drop a house on the witch.

Step two: live happily ever after,'" she said in a big, sarcastic voice.

"And we've lived right next to her our whole lives?" Tommy asked incredulously. "Next to an actual *witch?*"

A strained look came over Carmen's face. She was more worried about the part of the article that talked about mind-controlling the townspeople. She looked at her brother. "I think we need to follow Dad."

"Why?"

"Because we've both seen how strange everyone's been acting. But most of them just look cranky or distracted. And Dad seems different. It's almost like sometimes his actions aren't his own, like someone's..."

"...Mind-controlling him," Tommy supplemented, his eyes growing wide at the realization.

— — —

They snuck across the vehicle pool behind the police station, keeping their eyes peeled for any officers walking nearby. They found their father's cruiser parked in his main spot, and they tried one of the back doors, elated to see that it was unlocked.

"Come on," Carmen said to her brother, and he climbed into the car. She joined him, then she shut the door quietly behind her. Their father had some old boots, a big work bag, and a large jacket strewn across the back, and they lay themselves as close to the floor as they could get, covering themselves with all of the junk.

"Do you think he's gonna come anytime soon?" Tommy asked, coming straight to the important question.

"I hope so," she said.

They both waited, quickly growing uncomfortable as their bodies were twisted into odd shapes. It became harder to breathe for them under all of that stuff, but at least their breaths warmed up the car a bit. Carmen twisted her neck up and could just see out of the window from where she was. She watched as the clouds rolled by the gray sky and they listened to the faint sounds outside.

After an interminable amount of time, they heard footsteps approaching the car.

"Is that him?" Tommy asked.

But Carmen didn't dare move. "Stay still!" she commanded.

The driver's door of the cruiser opened and a heavy weight shifted inside. The door shut. Then the engine turned over and the car chugged into life. They felt themselves backing up. When the car pulled forward, Carmen slowly pressed herself up, making sure that the items on top of her didn't roll to the side and make noise. She rose just enough so that she could peek through the bottom of the cage separating the back from the front of the cruiser and see the driver. She saw the back of his short brown hair, and the edge of his trimmed mustache from the side. It was definitely their father. The question was: where was he going?

Carmen sank down and tapped her brother on the shoulder. He twisted his neck around to look at her, and she nodded. He nodded back, and they both waited, trying not to breathe too heavily.

The car seemed to roll along various roads forever. They had no idea what direction they were going in, or even if they were still in the same town. Time turned into a nebulous concept as they each stared at the carpet on the floor of the cruiser. Their bones and muscles ached. Their father remained dead silent as he drove the car; usually on a normal day he would be humming, but he wasn't normal anymore, and they wanted to find out how to fix that.

The road underneath the car suddenly got bumpy, and Robert decreased their speed. Then they hit a steep incline, and Carmen and Tommy rolled back against the edge of the footwells as the items on top of them slid. The ground was especially rocky now, and they both knew that they weren't on a normal road anymore. But where were they going?

The cruiser slowed to a crawl as it rumbled over each bump in the ground. It maneuvered widely around unseen obstacles. Eventually, the car stopped. They heard the gears shifting, and then the ignition was killed. The door opened and the weight shifted out of the car. The door slammed. The trunk opened. Then the trunk shut.

Carmen and Tommy looked at each other, still holding their breath. Carmen twisted up and looked out the window, seeing sky and tree branches now. When enough time had passed, and they thought they were in the clear, they slowly got up, timidly peeking out the windows.

They were in the woods. And the remains of Halloween House stood in front of them.

— CHAPTER FIFTEEN —

SPECIAL DELIVERY

Wendy Downsborough walked in the door of her house, and set down her work bag. She kicked off her shoes and walked into her living room, rubbing her temples. The babysitter spotted her and came into the living room.

"She's been an absolute angel," the teen in the baggy jeans and baseball cap said.

The woman looked at him suspiciously, but she didn't feel like nagging at him today for another poor job; she had been in a pinch when her boss called her in the morning and told her that three of her coworkers didn't show up to work. So she took out her wallet and paid him in cash, then he smiled and took off.

Wendy walked into her kitchen and poured herself a glass of water, slowly drinking it. She needed to put her feet up and do it soon, but not before checking on her daughter to make sure everything was all right.

When she drained the glass and put it in the sink, she headed to her daughter's bedroom. She pushed the door open and saw Caroline sitting on the bed, playing with her dolls. She looked up at her mom. "Hi, Mommy!" she said.

"Hi, Baby," Wendy said back, scrunching up her face and desperately trying to relieve the pressure behind her eyes. "Did you have a good day today?"

Caroline nodded up and down vigorously. She dropped one doll and picked up the gingerbread cookie sitting next to her, taking a bite.

Wendy looked at her suspiciously. "Where did you get that? Did Jack give you that today?"

Caroline shook her head. "The woman gave it to me."

"What woman?"

Caroline shrugged, then went back to playing with her dolls.

Wendy looked at the cookie sitting next to her. Alarm bells were going off in her head. She didn't at all understand what her daughter meant by that, and as a mother she should have taken the cookie away and investigated further, but right now she just couldn't summon the energy to do so. She was too irritated to think about it anymore, so she walked back to the living room and left her daughter alone. She lay down on the couch and put her feet up, just lying there and closing her eyes, letting her body fall into a nice rest.

A window squeaked open somewhere in the house.

Wendy's eyes opened. She wrestled with herself, but she decided to get up. She returned down the hallway to her daughter's room when suddenly the door opened. Caroline walked out of her room with a smile, and she passed her mother to the kitchen to get a drink. Wendy watched her go, then she turned her attention back to the bedroom. She pushed her way past the door and looked at the window, but it was closed, and the drapes were shut. The muted fear rising in her chest subsided, and she calmed down.

Caroline screamed at the other end of the house.

Wendy rushed into the hallway and saw her daughter standing at the other end. Caroline's feet were suddenly swept out from underneath her, and she fell to the carpet. Her arms splayed out in front of her and she was dragged out of view, screaming the entire way.

"Caroline!" Wendy shouted. She ran down the hallway into the living room just in time to see a flash of billowing, black robes sweep out of the window as her daughter's screams faded in the distance. She ran up to the window and stuck her head out, frantically looking around the neighborhood, but it was a calm, clear scene, and her daughter was nowhere in sight.

Her rapid heartbeat slowly subsided. She turned and looked at the front door, inspecting the doorknob like it was some strange and foreign device. Mostly, she was just trying to decide whether she wanted to use it or not. She glanced over her shoulder at the phone. There seemed to be some kind of customary ritual to these situations, but the practice of it was too vague in her head right now, and she was very tired.

She walked back to the couch and lay down again, putting her feet up and closing her eyes. Finally, she could get some good rest.

"I don't see him!" Tommy said, peeking out the window.

Carmen took a second opinion, and she agreed. "Okay, let's get out."

She carefully pushed open the door and they both crawled out of the back of the cruiser. She gingerly shut it behind her, holding the handle up until it was firmly against the frame before letting go of it.

The fire had consumed almost half of the house, vanquishing a large portion of the front-left section completely and leaving the rest of it as a burnt husk, a twisted mockery of what it used to be.

They skirted around to the side of the house that was more intact, gazing at the rubble of blackened wood and furniture that littered the front entrance. There was a window on the side of the house that looked in on the ground floor, and there were thin windows peering down into the basement.

The woods were chilly, and they both shivered, despite bundling themselves up in their thick coats. Their hearts raced, and everything around them, even in the starkness of the day, seemed spooky. Neither one of them had ever come up to this house, only hearing about it. They tried to imagine the locations of everything that they'd heard about, like it was playing out in front of them now. Tommy saw the jack-o'-lanterns surrounding the house, and Carmen turned her head and saw the witch chasing Peter through the woods.

They approached the window looking in at the ground floor in fear, like gazing into it would reveal some terrible secret that they weren't equipped to see. They avoided the basement windows in case Robert was down there and could see them. They pressed their hands to the charred wooden exterior apprehensively, as if even touching the house would place a hex on them. Then they sidled along, shoulder to shoulder, and they both peeked through the window in unison.

The house was not large, and only appeared to be comprised of a few small rooms. Some of the rooms was still wholly intact, and the other two only partially, the one at the front being almost completely wiped away by the fire. Dark piles of wood and old rubbish stood tall in front of them, and they could see through a slanted doorway to their right that led to a small and narrow room. And through the doorway, they could see a set of stairs leading down to the basement. But they didn't see their father. That meant...

They backed away from the window and went for one of the basement windows, careful to stay out of view from them. They crouched on the ground and leaned over, peeking inside, their hearts hammering and their mouths dry. The anticipation of what they would see built in their chests like a painful swell of gas.

The engine of the police cruiser roared into life.

Their heads snapped to the side and they saw the car back up between the trees, then make a wide turn and head down the steep hill.

"Hey!" Tommy cried. "How are we going to get back?"

Carmen's heart lurched. He was right. How *were* they going to get back?

"What do we do?"

She tried not to be a panic, because she didn't want her brother to do the same. Especially when they were at this house of all places, that was the last thing they needed. She took a deep breath. "Well, my dear brother," she said, trying to sound as calm as possible, "when faced with a dangerous situation, make the best of it. That's what any good adventurer would do."

Her trick seemed to work, as Tommy's face faded from fright into curiosity. "You're right," he said. "We're already here; we may as well take a look in the house."

They strode away from the house first, watching their father disappear down the hill. What had he been doing here? They hadn't been able to see, but he took something out of the trunk and disappeared into the house. Whatever he brought here, they would be able to find.

Carmen looked up at the sky, and the day was completely overcast, so it was impossible to tell how close to darkness it was. She reached into her pocket to pull out her cell phone, but her pocket was empty. "Oh no," she said.

"What?"

"I think I dropped my phone in Dad's cruiser."

Tommy's eyes widened.

"He's going to know."

Tommy turned his head to the house. "Well, it doesn't matter now. Dad doesn't seem to care, anyway."

She regarded her brother with sadness. But maybe he was right.

They turned back to the house, standing in front of its miserable and damaged façade. The front door had been wiped away by the damage, with only a small fragment of the frame remaining. They walked up the dilapidated porch, feeling like they were on hallowed ground, but not the good kind. They both stopped, looking at each other apprehensively and squeezing each other's hands.

"Okay," Carmen said simply, and then they stepped in to what was left of the house.

Even years later, there was an offensive smell that climbed up into their nostrils from the wreckage. Whatever strange items, mold, and exotic concoctions the witch had concealed had been fused to the ruins that remained. It was a horrible, nauseating scent, and the two of them did their best to ignore it as they carefully stepped over the rubble. They looked around, but there was really nothing to see, at least on the ground floor. They walked through what was left of the doorway into the main room they'd seen through the window at the middle of the house. What the room used to be, they couldn't even guess. It looked like there was a bed buried under a pile of long-dried black sludge, but it was hard to tell if they were seeing a warped frame, or a thick and wiry tree branch.

"I don't suppose you carry a pair of latex gloves on you, do you?" Carmen asked.

"Nope."

If they were looking for whatever it was their father delivered, they felt like it wouldn't be hard to spot it in this mess; it would be the only thing that wasn't burnt to an absolute crisp. And as they walked through the small spaces, they both had a feeling that whatever they were looking for was in the basement.

They crossed through the next doorway and saw the set of stairs leading down. The room they were in seemed to be a kitchen, with an old oven that was the only thing still intact from the blaze. They stopped to peer inside the door, but it was empty.

The darkness from the basement called up to them seductively, inviting them down.

Their skin crawled at the sight of it and they both couldn't help but imagine falling into a trap down there.

"Do you want to go first?" Tommy asked.

Carmen looked at him. "After you, Mr. Joe Hardy."

Tommy gulped. He stood at the top of the stairs and stared into the black. There was a faint bit of light coming in through the basement windows, but the area was mostly shrouded in shadow, and Carmen didn't even have her phone to light their way anymore.

Tommy lifted his foot and held onto the twisted husk of a railing as he started to lower himself down. But Carmen stepped in front of him and pushed him out of the way.

"I'm just kidding," she said. "I would never let you go first in a place like this."

He stared up at his big sister, wanting to save his honor, but right now he was glad to hear her say that.

Carmen started down the stairs, and each one groaned horribly, sinking a good inch or two under her weight. She felt like they were going to snap at any moment and she would plummet to her death, or at least a painful injury. But she went slowly and kept telling herself that everything was going to be fine. Tommy followed behind her, and the two of them sank down into the musty basement.

They reached the bottom without incident, and Carmen looked to her side, terribly afraid that she was going to see a bunch of children tied up or worse.

But there was nothing of the sort. The basement of the house had been affected by the blaze, but was still largely intact, as the fire mainly stayed on the ground floor. But everything was still scorched, and it was hard to see anything other than blackness in the dim light that was filtering through the narrow windows above them.

The room they were in was pretty bare, with only a few pieces of old furniture and some junk strewn around. A doorway stood ahead of them, and judging from the size of the house upstairs compared to the room they were in, they felt like this would be the final room of the basement and the entire house—the one stone left unturned.

They crept forward across the creaking floorboards, holding onto the cold cement wall next to them for support. The doorway loomed ahead of them, and they could only imagine what was waiting for them. They stepped through.

A long, heavy table sat in the middle of the room, and an old, large fireplace was perched in the back wall. Some splintered, shriveled firewood was nestled in it, but they both knew that it hadn't been used in years. Odd trinkets and decorations covered the walls, similar to Peter's house, but these were of a much darker sort.

However, aside from some other random junk and a couple of small pieces of furniture, there was nothing around to see. No children, no witch, no nothing.

Carmen and Tommy were almost disappointed as they looked around, expecting something more, expecting some kind of dazzling surprise from the mystery that had been built up. It seemed like Peter's suspicions were correct: wherever the witch was, if she even had an actual hideout anymore, it wasn't here. And neither were the children. So then what was going on?

The two of them were about to leave, when suddenly Tommy spotted something in the corner of his eye. He tugged on his sister's sleeve, and he crouched down, peering underneath the table. The surface of it was so wide and thick that it was hard to see beneath it, even from the doorway. But as Carmen bent down, she saw that there was a thin shelf underneath. And sitting on that shelf was a cardboard box, the kind that someone would pack their cubicle up with when they were fired. It was the only object in the entire house that wasn't scorched black.

"That must be what Dad brought!" Carmen said. They both rushed over to it and Carmen picked it up and placed it on top of the table. She held her hands on either side of the lid, suddenly too frightened to open it.

Tommy looked at his sister. "Well? Open it!" he urged.

But she looked at him with uncertainty. "What if we really don't want to see what's inside?"

The possibility hit him hard, and suddenly the excitement was washed off his face. He understood her point; what was their father doing here of all places, bringing a box? Whatever it was, it couldn't be good.

But with this in mind, Carmen knew the best thing to do was to press forward and find out what was going on. She took a deep breath and then she lifted the lid, setting it aside.

The box seemed to be filled with rags or cloth of some sort, and Carmen cautiously lowered her hands into it and began rummaging around.

"Ew!" she cried, pulling her hand out. She held it up to the faint light coming in through a basement window and saw that some kind of goop covered her fingers. "Oh, what *is* that?"

Tommy leaned forward and peered in the box. He stuck his finger in and pulled it out, inspecting the slime.

"No, don't you touch it, too!" Carmen said. "Just stand back." She reached in again more cautiously, wiping the goop on the rags inside. She tried another section of the box and pulled her hand out again. "That was a bug," she said miserably. "A dead bug." Her face scrunched up in disgust.

Tommy stepped forward and rummaged around against her wishes. He pulled out his magnifying glass. "Dead cockroaches," he pronounced. "And beetles. Grasshoppers, too." He sorted through, pulling out fresh weeds and flowers. His hand dipped into the box again, and his thumb and forefinger closed on something, slowly drawing it out. It was long and stringy, and as they both stared at it, they realized it was a shoelace.

It pulled taut, and Tommy reached down and retrieved the other end of it in horror. A child-sized shoe came out of the box underneath the rags, then Tommy searched again and pulled out a different shoe.

"Wait a minute..." Carmen said, shivering. She pulled out the rags at the top of the box and unfolded them.

They weren't rags at all; they were clothes. Children's clothes.

"Oh no..." Carmen said. "No, no, no... What's Dad doing with this stuff?"

Tommy stepped back. "Did dad... hurt them?"

Carmen snapped her head to him. "No! Tommy, don't think that. Dad would never do something like that. He's not himself right now. All he did was deliver this box." She looked back inside, pulling out more clothes with a heavy heart. All she wanted to know was where he got all this.

"Wait..." Tommy said. "I recognize this stuff." He pulled out some of the weeds and flowers.

"Where's it from?" Carmen asked.

"The church at the edge of town," he said. "That's where the children are."

— CHAPTER SIXTEEN —

IN TRANSIT

The blackened husk of Halloween House stood behind them at the top of the hill as they made their way down through the woods. Tommy occasionally glanced over his shoulder at it, expecting it to march after them and gobble them up. He shivered at the thought.

The sky started to dim on their way down, and they knew it would still be a while before they made it back to residential streets. This scared Carmen the most. She hadn't expected her father to drive them out so far, and she wasn't sure they would make it back in time before dark. But she tried to keep her brother's spirits up.

"It's not much further," she said.

He stared in the distance ahead of them, trying to cut an arrow of vision through the trees and see something—anything—that he recognized. But he couldn't. He swallowed a lump down his throat, and he kept moving.

Their legs were sore, and they were both filled with a lot of questions. They were certain they'd figured out where the children were being kept, if they were still alive. Tommy remembered that the timothy-grass grew in a little marsh of water at the edge of the church's property, and he recalled when their father and mother would take him and his sister up there on special occasions and he would play around in the flower gardens. But it had been a long time since he'd been there—not since their mom died, in fact—and those were only distant memories. But they had to be right. The only question was, would Peter be able to help them do something to save the kids? Or to defeat the witch? The thought seemed ludicrous to them.

Carmen's heart sank at the same rate as the sun did, and by the time they neared the edge of the woods, the sun dipped down over the horizon completely, giving the night dominion over them.

They made it to Lansdowne Road, about the farthest road as they could get from their home. Carmen rubbed her hands together for warmth, putting them up to her mouth and blowing on her cold fingers. Then she took her brother's hands and warmed them up too. He gave her a look as if to ask if they were going to make it, and her own look told him that she didn't know. She didn't want to have to travel back home on foot, and the thought of holing up somewhere else for the night was frightening, to say the least. But she had an idea.

She figured it must have been about 7:30 or so, and she was sure that there would be a bus coming down the road on Berryman soon. That would take them most of the way home. From there, it was only a few blocks. And then in the morning they could get up bright and early and head to the school to meet up with Peter.

The streets were mostly empty, but there were still a few cars driving around. They were in a residential area, so there weren't many people on foot, and they were glad for it. When they got to Berryman, they made their way to the bus stop and hunkered inside of the shelter, grateful for the glass walls that shielded them from the wind.

They stared through them down the road, watching the traffic lights change from red to green and back again. The occasional car would putter along in the distance, and they watched the wildlife moving around with a careful eye. But everything seemed peaceful tonight.

Headlights shined in the distance. They both looked over at them and saw that they belonged to the number eleven bus. Carmen fished around in her pocket for some change, and she clutched it in her hand. The bus arrived and pulled to a stop next to them with a whine of the brakes. The doors opened, and the driver peered down at them, his eyes cold as ice.

"Evening," Carmen said quietly as she boarded the bus and dropped the coins in the slot. Tommy followed after her, keeping his eyes on the floor.

The bus driver close the doors and eased onto the accelerator.

Carmen and Tommy moved down the aisle, holding onto the handrails on the way to steady themselves until they found a seat. The bus was unusually packed, but they spotted two empty seats toward the rear.

The eyes of every person sitting there fell on them as they moved. No one talked; they just stared. The bus rumbled and gently swayed from side to side over bumps in the road. The two of them found their seats, and they tucked their knees together, sitting quietly with their hands in their laps.

Most of the eyes wandered back to their normal spots, but often someone would turn their head to look at them directly.

"*Why are they staring at us?*" Tommy whispered.

"*Shh!*" Carmen said.

Someone in the middle of the bus started talking, and the sound of a voice cutting through the silence was so alarming that Carmen couldn't help but jump in her seat. It belonged to an older man who looked to be in his sixties, a tight baseball cap clamped to his head. His head was turned, and he was looking at another passenger. Carmen and Tommy couldn't hear what he was saying, but the look in his eyes said it all.

The man he was talking to was a younger man, maybe in his thirties. He was a large, hulking man with a shaved head and a big beard. Neither of the men looked pleasant, and they certainly didn't look friendly to each other. The other man talked back, and both of their voices rose in volume. Everyone else's eyes fell on them, and soon the first, thinner man stood up and marched to the other one. Normally such a sight would never be seen, but the man was fearless. He punched the larger man in the face.

Carmen put a hand to her mouth in shock. Her brother started in the seat, just as surprised as she was.

The larger man didn't take kindly to it, and in the next moment he shot up to his feet, grabbing the man by the collar and barreling through him along the aisle. The man crashed across the laps of two passengers sitting near the front of the bus, and they all cried out in pain.

The bus driver stared at the scene in his rearview mirror, his gentle touch on the wheel starting to veer.

More people joined the melee, and those who didn't threw their voices into the fray in anger. The scene quickly devolved into chaos as more people stood up and moved to the middle of the bus, brawling with each other.

Carmen and Tommy ducked in their seats, trying to wedge themselves down and make themselves a small as possible so they didn't become a target, didn't even provoke the notice of anyone. "Just stay down," she told him. "Just stay down and wait."

The bus driver became increasingly distracted as he watched the chaos behind him. Then the ruckus came to him as a man was shoved into the driver. The driver's arm was yanked, and the wheel veered along with it. The bus swerved to the side violently before the driver was able to correct it. Everyone was thrown to the left, and Carmen and Tommy held on for dear life so they wouldn't be flung out of their seats.

Fists were thrown, blood was spilt, teeth flew, and obscenities were hurled as the brawl turned into an all-out dog pile. It spoke to more than just anger; this was pure rage. The townspeople were pushed past the brink, and their fear had been their undoing, giving their power over to the witch and tearing themselves apart.

"Stay calm," Carmen whispered to Tommy. "Stay calm." He hunkered down, his eyes wide with fear. Eventually he snapped his eyes shut, not wanting to look at the chaos anymore.

The driver was distracted again and the bus veered once more. It sideswiped a car parked on the road and the driver swung the wheel the other way to correct. But he overcorrected and the bus fishtailed. The hulking mass swerved from side to side on the road, then another car parked on the other side of the street was swiped. Hot sparks splashed into the night as the people inside tumbled around.

The bus caught a hard turn and Tommy was flung out of his seat.

"Tommy!" Carmen cried.

He stumbled across the aisle and reached up, grabbing the top of a seat while his body flailed like a minnow caught on a fishing line. The bus changed direction, and he was thrown into a new seat across the aisle from Carmen.

The driver lost control completely and the bus headed off the road for a ditch. The wheels sailed over the grass, and the bus came down hard at the bottom of the dip, crashing down on the suspension and compressing everyone's spines. It knocked the wind out of them, and Carmen gasped for breath as the bus hurtled into a tree. The front of it crunched against the thick trunk and caused the back end of the bus to lift off the ground several feet, spin around in the air and crash down onto the wheels, tossing everyone inside around like rag dolls. Finally, the bus's center of balance tipped over and it crashed on its side with a thunderous bang. It glided along the grass for a few yards, then it came to rest.

When Carmen looked up, her head was spinning and she saw stars. She groaned. Tommy groaned, too, and she realized that he was lying on top of her. When she could summon the strength, she reached over and shook his elbow. "Tommy? Are you okay?"

He groaned again.

"Can you move? You have to move."

Carmen crawled out from under him. She didn't know if she was injured, but she couldn't worry about that now; they were in a crashed and overturned bus, surrounded by the mad and deranged townspeople. If they didn't want to die here tonight, they had to get out now. She pulled herself up enough to peek over the seats into the aisle. The whole bus looked strange now from her new perspective, and she had trouble figuring out which way was which.

They obviously wouldn't be able to break out of the windows underneath them, and the ones on the other side—which were above them now—seemed too far away and inaccessible to get through. That only left the front of the bus where the door was.

The people in the bus began to stir, each of them groaning. Some of them started crying out in pain, either from the brawl or from the crash. The driver was slumped against the side of the bus next to the wheel, motionless.

"Come on, we have to go!" Carmen urged. Her brother continued to groan, but she forced him up, terrified that he had broken something. He held an arm to his stomach as she raised him to his feet, but he held his own footing, and at least those weren't broken.

"My stomach hurts," he complained.

"Don't worry about that now," she said. "We have to go for the door!"

He was slow and cumbersome, but he worked with her, and she guided the two of them over the pile of groaning and wriggling bodies to get to the front. Their footing was uneven as everyone moved underneath them, but they held onto whatever they could to get by. Tommy whined quietly under his breath as he walked, his face scrunched up in pain. But Carmen didn't see any blood on him, and she hoped that he had just been hit in the stomach by something.

He got halfway through the bus, then the big, lumbering man who'd got punched in the first place, rolled over and grabbed Tommy by the ankle.

Tommy tripped and fell down on the bodies.

Carmen spun around. "Tommy!" She grabbed her brother by the wrists, trying to pull him, but the man wouldn't let go.

"Help me!" Tommy cried, looking behind at the man and trying to kick at him to free himself. But the man's grip was like iron.

"That's a kid!" Carmen shrieked. "He's just a little kid, you freak!" Carmen struggled, trying to pull her brother with all her might, but the man easily drew Tommy closer to him with strong and measured yanks.

The thin man with the baseball cap who'd started the fight was roused and shook the stars out of his head, then in the next moment he jumped on the big man and put his hands on his throat, choking the breath out of him. This distracted the large man enough to let go of Tommy, and he and Carmen stumbled toward the front of the bus from the strength by which she was pulling him.

They scrambled the rest of the way, and Carmen helped Tommy stand on the wall surrounding the incapacitated driver. She pulled the lever, which opened the doors above them, then she hoisted her brother up and he slowly climbed onto the top of the bus. She jumped up, grabbing onto the open door and holding onto anything she could as she struggled to pull up her weight. Tommy tried to help her on top, and eventually she got free. They found the closest, softest patch of grass they could find, and they jumped down, safely outside of the bus.

"Are you okay?" Carmen asked Tommy.

He nodded, feeling a little bit better. He lifted up his shirt, and his stomach had the start of a bruise on it, but it didn't seem like the damage was too bad. "I feel better," he said. "I think something just hit me."

Carmen tossed a glance at the bus. "We have to get out of here before they start getting out."

Tommy agreed and they hurried back up to the sidewalk along the road. The bus had run down into a ditch with a long stretch of woods on the other side of it from the road. They kept to the sidewalk, heading straight down, and Carmen thought that would take them home.

There was a storm tunnel up ahead where water trickled out into the ditch in a steady rhythm. The breeze fluttered through the air, brushing across their exposed skin and gliding up through the trees, making them sway.

Carmen looked up at the trees at the edge of the woods and for some reason they looked funny to her. She gazed at them carefully, trying to understand what she was seeing, and when she did, her heart stopped.

The trees were filled with bats, hanging upside down and sleeping.

Tommy must have seen the look on her face, because he looked up at the trees too, and he screamed.

The bats' eyes opened in unison, hundreds of them, maybe thousands of them. They screeched, and the wretched sounds filled the sky.

"Run!" Carmen screamed. She and Tommy took off down the sidewalk as the bats spread their wings and plunged off of their perches. They searched around frantically, but across the bare street, there were only commercial buildings which were locked for the night.

The bats closed in, gliding effortlessly through the sky toward them, and Carmen and Tommy knew they would be picked apart if they didn't find somewhere to hide.

The storm tunnel approached like a dark but welcoming beacon. They didn't have any choice. They ran for it.

— CHAPTER SEVENTEEN —

THE TUNNELS

The bats swooped down and mercilessly attacked them. They shielded their faces and flailed their arms around, trying to hold off the offensive. The bottom of the tunnel was filled with a shallow layer of water, and their feet splashed through it as they tried to escape. The water made it hard for them to run, and Carmen tripped and fell to her knees, a big splash of water launching up and soaking her. A hundred tiny wings slapped against her and she felt stinging bites against the back of her neck. She screamed and got back up to her feet, flailing around.

"Come on!" Tommy urged, running ahead of her.

They fled deeper into the tunnel, which was lit up with bright work lights on either side that were spaced out periodically.

Once they got far enough in, the bulk of the bats gave up their pursuit, either turning and flying out of the tunnel, or taking a temporary refuge inside, turning upside down and clinging to the ceiling and blocking their escape.

Carmen and Tommy came to a junction and the tunnel stretched off ahead of them in two different directions. They stopped. Carmen spun around and stared down the tunnel they'd come through. Her eyes were wide and her chest heaved in and out. It felt like the bats were still attacking her, but that was just the residual stinging pain she was feeling.

Tommy was bitten too, but not as badly as Carmen. "How does it look?" she asked him. She bent down and he walked around her, looking at the damage on her neck. "Ow!" she said as his fingers touched her wounds.

"It's not too bad," Tommy said, giving his honest opinion. "You're bleeding a little bit, but I think you'll be okay."

She trusted his opinion and she settled down a little. "Let me have a look at you," she said, reaching out for him. He stepped forward and she spun him around, inspecting the back of his neck and his hands. He had a couple of cuts, but nothing to worry about. She feared that some of the bats could have rabies, but there would be nothing they could do about that now, anyway. The only thing they needed to focus on was finding a way out of here. Carmen lifted his shirt and looked at his torso, seeing the bruise forming over his stomach. She gently pressed her fingers around his ribs. "Does this hurt?" she asked.

He grimaced. "Yeah. Are they broken?"

She judged based on his reaction and how much pressure she used, and she said, "No, maybe just bruised."

"Help!"

Carmen and Tommy looked down one of the new pathways. A distant voice echoed off the walls, and they both heard it.

"Help!" the voice said again, and they both recognized it.

"Who is that?" Carmen said.

They looked at each of the two tunnels, trying to figure where it had come from, but being in such an enclosed space played strange tricks on the sound.

"I think it came from here," Tommy said, picking the right path. Carmen held his hand and they went down it, splashing through the water.

When they slowed down, they could hear frantic sloshing somewhere else in the system of storm tunnels. There was another junction up ahead and they picked up the pace. When they got to it, they collided right into someone else, and the three of them were knocked backward and fell into the water.

They all saw stars, and when they regained their composure and got up, they stared at each other in the stark light.

It was Shawn. "Tommy... What are you doing here?"

"We were attacked by bats and chased into here," he said. "Why are you here?"

"Same," Shawn said. "I was with Brett and Randy, and after the bats attacked us, we all kinda split up. Brett went somewhere else, and Randy and I ran in here. But I think there's something else in here following us."

"The witch," Tommy said, barely above a whisper.

Shawn's eyes widened. "Shh! Don't say that!"

"Where's Randy?" Carmen asked, cutting in.

"Help!" the voice came again, and they all snapped their heads toward the tunnel.

"We were attacked in here, and we split up," Shawn explained. "All I saw was black robes walking through the tunnel for us. But it wasn't really walking, it was like it was floating." He paused, then he added, "But don't say witch! Don't say witch, don't say witch..."

Carmen clapped a hand on his shoulder and brought him back to reality. "We need to get your friend and get out of here," she told him.

"Right," Shawn said. He looked over his shoulder. "I think he's somewhere down this way." Shawn pointed the way and Carmen and Tommy followed him. They worked their way through the tunnels, often coming up to various branching paths. They relied on Shawn's instincts, having already been trapped in the tunnel for a little while, and they also utilized Randy's frantic movements and cries to pinpoint his location.

"Randy!" Shawn cried.

"Over here!" Randy shouted. "Oh God, man! I think she's coming for me!"

The three of them came to another junction, and they looked down the path to the left, hearing Randy's noises very close now. They stopped and watched as hurried footsteps approach them. Around the corner, Randy popped into view, running as fast as he could for them. "She's coming!" he cried. The three of them watched in horror and fascination at the end of the tunnel behind him, waiting to see something. But nothing was chasing him. Randy got closer and closer to them, and in a few more strides, he would reach them.

And then the witch came into view, gliding over the water and moving faster than any of them could. Her figure was short and stocky, but she moved with an incredibly lithe agility. Her face was hidden underneath her wide black hat, but her long, stringy white hair flowed out and it slowly fluttered from side to side in the air as she moved, like the laws of physics had no effect on her. The only other part of her that could be seen were her hands. They were pale, almost translucent. In one of them she held a short, gnarled length of wood.

The three of them that were standing still immediately turned and ran as Randy caught up to them in midstride. From behind them, the witch pointed the thin length of wood at them and shrieked something.

Suddenly the lights in the tunnel went out one by one, quickly catching up to and overcoming them until they were left in blackness. Their loss of vision caused them to stumble and slow down, and the fact that they couldn't even hear the witch moving through the water behind them made everything all the more terrifying. The four of them held their hands out to stop them from slamming into a wall. They attempted to stay together, but it was hard to tell where they were in the dark.

"I see lights!" Randy shouted. And so did the rest of them. They ran for it, still not knowing how close the witch was, and when they came to a brightly-lit four-way intersection, Carmen stopped and turned around.

The others followed. The tunnel they'd just come through was completely lit up now, and there was no sign of the witch anywhere. Each of the four of them looked down a different tunnel, keeping their backs to each other.

"I don't see her," Tommy said.

"She's out there!" Randy said, softly bouncing up and down on the spot. "I'm telling you, man! She's out there!"

The four of them backed up slowly, their heels dragging through the water. As they all closed to within a foot of each other, they heard the sound of bubbling water. They each stared even more intensely down their respective tunnels, but still they couldn't see anything.

"Where's that coming from?" Randy shouted.

"Um, guys?" Shawn said.

They all turned around to look at him, and then they saw that he was staring down at the small patch of water between them.

The water bubbled for seemingly no reason, like it had been brought to a boil. A frog leapt out from under the surface, jumping high and bouncing off Tommy's chest. Tommy stumbled backward into the wall in surprise, and another frog leapt out of the water, then another. Soon, the bubbling surface was covered more in frogs than water as hundreds of them were dredged up, jumping out at them like popcorn. The four of them backed up as the frogs continued to multiply. Then the amphibians rose into the air as the witch stretched up from underneath the surface of the water.

"Run!" Carmen shouted. Tommy turned to sprint in the opposite direction, but Carmen grabbed his arm and pulled him toward her. She took off down the tunnel with her brother's arm in her hand, and Randy and Shawn split off in other directions. They fled through the maze, taking paths at random, and still not seeing a way out. Carmen came up to another junction and turned down the left path. But it only went for a little ways before the rest of the path was blocked off by a set of iron bars. Shawn rounded the corner on the other side and came up to them.

The witch followed, and he spun around and pressed his back to the bars.

"No!" he shouted. Shawn turned and tried to slip through the bars, but the space between them was too narrow. Tommy and Carmen tried to pull him through, but he just got stuck. In the flash of an eye, Shawn's feet were pulled out from under him and his body hit the water with a mighty splash. Then the witch took off with him at an incredible speed as his body hydroplaned through the water and whipped around the corner out of view, his screams trailing off in the distance.

"Come on!" Carmen said, pulling Tommy by the shoulders. They turned around and went to the other end of the tunnel they were in. They came up to a junction at the end of it and Randy sped by from the right.

"A ladder! I see it!" he cried, pointing. Carmen and Tommy followed him and when they reached the bottom of it, they all stopped and looked up. The ladder led to a manhole, and the three of them saw their salvation.

Randy turned and looked down the tunnel they'd come from and yelped when he saw the witch gliding toward them.

"I'll open it!" Carmen said, then she started climbing the ladder. Tommy was right on her heels, and Randy behind him. When she reached the top, she braced herself against the rungs, then she pushed up on the manhole cover. It was incredibly heavy, and at first her heart sank, thinking that it wouldn't budge at all, but she stepped up to the next rung to get more leverage and she pushed her legs and her shoulder into it as hard as she could. It slowly lifted and she nudged it to the side. When the edge of it was on the pavement above, she reached up and shoved it enough for them to slip through.

She climbed out of the sewer and found herself on Rosedale Avenue, not far from her house. She spun around on her hands and knees and looked down the hole. Tommy was almost to the top, but her heart leapt when she saw the witch come into view.

"Noooo!" Randy cried as he was yanked off the rungs and dragged through the water.

Tommy came up through the hole, then Carmen grabbed the edge of the cover and shoved with all her might to put it back into place. She stood up and grabbed her brother's hand, then they ran home.

They nearly crashed through the front door, and Carmen slammed it behind them and locked it. They looked around, but their father wasn't home. Still soaking wet and reeking of mold and mildew, the two of them went to the bathroom and took turns changing out of their clothes and showering, putting on their pajamas and trying to settle in for the night.

They both hid in Tommy's cubbyhole the entire night, Carmen clutching the witch mirror from Peter. They stayed awake for a long time, waiting to hear the front door open and hear the sound of their father's footsteps. But he never came home that night, and Carmen was glad for it. Eventually, when tiredness came over them, their eyes closed and they drifted off to sleep. They spent the entire night resting peacefully and undisturbed.

And so did the gingerbread man sitting on Tommy's windowsill outside.

— CHAPTER EIGHTEEN —

Jail Talk Redux

Carmen and Tommy stood in the school's parking lot, shivering in the morning light. They searched around, waiting for Peter to show up.

"Where is he?" Carmen muttered under her breath.

"Maybe he's not coming," Tommy said.

With each car that rolled down the road in front of them, their expectations rose, only to fall when they saw the blank expression on a random face, staring at the road as they drove.

Carmen glanced to the left and saw another car cutting down the road. When she saw what it was, her heart sank.

The police cruiser crept toward the school, then turned into the parking lot. Robert was behind the wheel, and he stared, expressionless, at his two children. He pulled the cruiser to a stop and put it into park, then he opened his door and stepped out.

"Are you waiting for someone?" Robert asked.

As soon as he said the words, Carmen knew immediately what happened. Peter had been taken and locked up again, and any help they were hoping to get from him to stop what was going on was completely dashed now.

"Come on, I'll take you two home," he said.

Tommy looked up at his sister, uncertainty swimming in his eyes.

"No," Carmen said. "We're not going with you."

"I insist," their father said. His eyes turned to Tommy, burning into him with a crazed intensity. "Tommy, too."

Tommy looked up at his sister again, a strained look on his face. He knew there was something wrong with his dad, but he was never one to disobey his direct authority. He took a step toward the car, but Carmen grabbed him and held him in place.

"You can take me," Carmen said. "Only me. Not Tommy." She turned to her brother and knelt down. "You go on home, okay?" she whispered. "Don't stop, don't talk to anyone, no matter what happens; just get home. Lock all the doors, hide, and stay there. I'll be back there as soon as I can."

"Where is he gonna take you?" Tommy asked, scared.

"Don't worry about me," she said, then she gave him a loving bop with her finger on the tip of his nose. She stood up and gave the back of his shoulders a shove. "Go," she said.

Tommy started to walk toward the schoolyard to cut across it and head home, but he only made it a few steps before he slowed down and looked between his sister and his father.

"Go!" Carmen said.

"Come on, son. Get in the car," Robert said, staring at him like he was a big meal.

Tommy was torn with indecision, but the look of determination on Carmen's face gave him the strength he needed to turn away from his father and run across the field. He didn't look back, and Carmen made sure that their father stayed put while he ran.

Robert watched him go, not taking his eyes off of him.

"Let's go, Dad." Carmen said. She walked over to the cruiser and climbed in the passenger door.

Robert stood there staring at Tommy for another few moments before he finally sank down into the driver's seat and closed the door.

"Take me to the station," Carmen insisted.

"I'll take you home," he said slowly.

"No, to the station. *Now*." Her words were slow and forceful.

Robert's face twisted into a grimace and he rubbed the back of his neck roughly. The moment of anguish painted on him lasted for a few more seconds, then it washed away and his eyes took on the familiar glazed-over look as he robotically drove Carmen to the police station.

Carmen subtly tried to twist around in her seat and look at the back seat through the cage for her cell phone. She didn't see it, and when she turned back around, Robert held it up in his hand.

His head swiveled toward her. "You dropped this," he said without emotion.

She considered him, then she timidly reached out and took her phone from him. She stared back at him, and she prepared an excuse, but he just stared straight ahead without a word for the rest of the ride.

When they got to the station, Carmen didn't wait for him to even pulled to a full stop; she got out of the car and rushed into the station, moving down the hallway to the jail cells.

"Hey, what are you doing in here!" the rotund officer said from behind his desk.

"Shut up!" Carmen said, rushing past him. She moved along the cells, looking in each one, and she found Peter lying on the cot in the same cell as he was before. Carmen turned her head to the side and saw the officer get up from his desk, but she gave him a vicious look and he sat back down.

"Carmen..." Peter said, noticing her. "What are you doing here?"

"I came to see you," she said, wrapping her hands around the bars. "What did they lock you up for?"

"They wouldn't say, but I can take a guess."

"So can I," she said. "Things are getting worse."

"Not much time now," he said.

"Did you find anything?"

Peter sat up and faced her. He stood and walked to the bars, pressing his face between them and twisting his neck to see if anyone else was nearby and listening in. There was a window high up in the wall just outside of his cell, and he eyed it suspiciously before he spoke.

"I think the witch is trying to regenerate herself," he said. "That's why she needs the children."

"Regenerate herself? Why?"

"She was killed," Peter explained, "but not fully. She's trapped in a limbo state between life and death. And now she's much weaker than she was when she was alive."

"*What?*"

"It sounds hard to believe," he continued, "but if you think she's powerful now, just imagine what she could do if she were restored to her full vitality. The only reason this town existed for so many years was because of her good graces to leave it well enough alone. But now the truce is broken, and she won't stop ever again. Children have the most potent lifeblood, and she needs them."

"My brother and I went to the house," Carmen said.

Peter's eyes widened. "*Her*... house?"

She nodded. "We followed my dad up there. He delivered a box to the house, but we don't know why. The whole place was empty, and when we looked in the box, we found children's clothing, and a bunch of other stuff like dead bugs and flowers and slime."

A flash of excitement crossed Peter's face. "That's what I thought," he said. "She's going to create a witch's brew."

"A what?"

"A witch's brew that she'll be making in her cauldron. That's what all of those items and ingredients are for; they're to infuse the mixture, and when she adds the children into it, it will literally turn into a life-giving potion to her. You can't let that happen."

"How am I supposed to stop her?" Carmen asked, exasperated. "It's not like you're much help, no offense."

"You have to find those children and figure out where she's going to do it tonight," he said. "And she *will* do it tonight on Halloween. I'm certain of it. It will be three years to the moment when she burned for a false crime, most likely."

"My brother and I think we know where they are," Carmen said. "When we saw those items in the box at the witch's house, Tommy recognized the flowers and weeds; they came from the church on the edge of town."

"I know the one," he said.

"That must be where they are. But if that's the case, why did my dad bring that box of things for the brew to her house? There was nothing there. We didn't see a cauldron."

Peter considered all of this. "Hmm, I don't know. But if you're certain the children are being kept at the church right now, you have to go there and save them."

"But how do I *do* that? I've seen this witch up close. I can't exactly fight her or just carry the children out of there."

He nodded. "That's right. You've got to arm yourself first, otherwise you're just going to be another one of her victims. You need to get some supplies, things that will protect yourself from her."

"Like what? I already have the mirror. How do I actually kill her? You know, once and for all?"

"Your best chance is to spike her witch's brew," Peter said.

"Spike it?"

"Yes, exactly. If you add a couple of ingredients to it—ingredients that witches are allergic to—and she doesn't know about it and drinks it, that should be enough to weaken if not kill her."

"And if it doesn't kill her?" Carmen asked warily.

"Well, you better pray it does," he said. "You might also want to find an iron weapon of some sort, like a knife. That by itself can be deadly to witches, at least the normal kind. If she's trapped as a wraith, like you've described already, I don't know how much effect it would have. She would need to have a more corporeal form for it to be useful."

Carmen went through these ideas in her head. "So what's she allergic to?"

"The most readily available things would be garlic and salt," he said. "If you put enough of that in there, it should be more than enough to incapacitate her."

"Garlic? I thought that was for vampires."

"Common misconception," he said. "Witches hate it, too."

Carmen took a step away from the bars and regarded Peter with a careful look. "Okay, I can find those things before tonight, but let's see if I have this straight... You're saying I need to wait until the witch starts making her brew tonight—AKA the last possible moment—to go and defeat her?"

"And if you're a moment later, all of the children will die. Yes, exactly."

"Okay, just making sure I got that right," Carmen said, shivering. "No problem at all."

— CHAPTER NINETEEN —

Pumpkin Patch

Carmen unlocked the front door to her house and stepped inside. She dropped the keys on the kitchen counter, then called out Tommy's name. She walked around the house a little, but she didn't hear him.

"Tommy, it's only me! There's no one else here. You can come out."

She waited, listening. A moment later, a closet door behind her opened, and she turned around to see her brother spill out from under a pile of blankets. He looked like he was gasping for air, and a thin layer of sweat coated his forehead and matted his hair to his face.

"Are you okay?" she asked, helping him up.

"Yeah," he said, "I was just in there for a while. What happened with you and Dad?"

"Nothing happened," she said. "I went and talked to Peter. They have them locked up."

"Is everything going to be okay? What did he say?"

Carmen led him into his bedroom and they sat on the edge of his bed, talking. Carmen held the witch mirror in her hands, turning it over and rubbing her thumb against the smooth stone.

"Peter can't help us," Carmen said, "and neither can anyone else. I have to go and stop the witch tonight myself."

"You mean *we* have to go, right?" he asked.

Carmen shook her head. "It's too dangerous for you," she replied. "I don't think the witch wants anything with me; she only wants children."

"Why?"

"Peter said it's because she needs them to regenerate back to her old form. She can get stronger that way."

"No," Tommy said, "I mean why wouldn't you let me go? Are you just going to leave me at home while you go do it?"

"It's safer that way," she said.

Tommy looked down at his feet, depressed.

Carmen gently placed her hand on his arm. "What's the matter?"

He sighed. "I never get to do anything. When Mom was still around—"

"Tommy," she interrupted, "now's not a good time to do the whole Mom guilt trip thing, okay?"

"No, I'm just saying," he continued, "when Mom was around, she made sure that we did everything we wanted and needed. Not just me, but you too. Even Dad. Ever since she died, Dad's just been getting busier and busier with work, and he doesn't spend time with me anymore. I'm not even talking about what's been happening lately, I just mean in general. You've had to pick up the slack a lot and spend more time with me, and I know sometimes you don't want to."

"Hey," she said, pulling him in for a hug, "of course I want to spend time with you."

"But you know what I mean, right?" he said. "If mom was still here, I would be going trick-or-treating, and I would be able to do other stuff, too, that Dad forgets about."

Carmen sighed. She felt sympathetic for her brother, but his safety was her paramount priority. Still, she saw the pained look in his eyes, the result of one too many disappointments, and she would give anything to put a smile on his face. She thought for a moment, trying to find a happy medium.

"I know," she said.

He lifted his head and looked at her.

"We never got your costume."

"Yeah, I know. What's your point?"

"My point is, why don't we get you one?" she said with a smile. "Do you want to be Joe Hardy?"

His eyes lit up. "Yeah... but how?"

"Well, you still got that old red sweater, don't you?" she asked.

He nodded.

"I can help you fix up the rest. Even if no one else knows who you are, you and I will, and that's all that matters."

"Okay," he said, "but what difference does it make if I can't go trick-or-treating? Randy and Shawn were already taken by the witch. It's too dangerous for me to go out at night."

"You can't go trick-or-treating," Carmen said, "but we can do something else fun today while it's still light out."

"What?"

"How would you like to go to the pumpkin patch?"

A smile slid across his face.

— — —

They arrived at the Sawyer family farm near the west end of town in mid-afternoon. Carmen was bundled up in her normal coat and jeans, and Tommy was dressed up with two layers of t-shirts underneath his red sweater. Carmen had used some old hair dye she had to change Tommy's hair to the particular shade of blond on his book covers, and she dressed him up as closely as possible to his favorite mystery novel icon.

The pumpkin patch was busy, with many parents walking around with their children. Everyone still seemed strange, but they didn't get too crazy in the daytime; only at night. Carmen would keep a watchful eye on her brother and make sure nothing happened to him, and in exchange he would get to have some fun for Halloween. Besides, she had an ulterior motive for coming here, anyway: she needed to prepare for tonight and get the items that Peter told her to gather. She had salt at home, but not garlic, nor anything made of iron that could be used as a weapon. But if anyone might have had that stuff, the Sawyer farm was a good bet, allowing her to kill a few birds with one stone.

"Why don't you go inside?" Carmen told Tommy, handing him the ticket that she bought. "I'm just going to go buy some garlic."

He nodded with a smile, turned, and skipped off for the girl standing at the admission gate.

A whole host of jack-o'-lanterns had greeted them on the way in, each one carved into a different funny or frightening face, and Carmen heard that at nighttime the farm owner put on quite a lights show with them. But she had absolutely no intention of sticking around until dark, and she feared for any of the other townspeople who did.

There was a stand before the admission gate where she could buy tickets or food, and there was also a large cart of locally-grown produce in addition to the huge boxes full of pumpkins for people to buy. She rummaged through it and found garlic. "Yes!" she said under her breath. "How much for this?" she asked, taking a bag full of five bulbs.

"Three dollars," the girl behind the counter grumbled.

Carmen took the money out of her pocket and handed it to her, then she took the garlic and stuffed it in her coat. With that on hand, she would just have to look for something made of iron while she kept an eye on Tommy and made sure he didn't stray too far. She headed for the admission gate.

Tommy had already skipped quite a ways ahead, excitedly looking around at all of the attractions. It had been quite a number of years since their mom took them here, and there were many new additions, like quite a few animatronic shows featuring jack-o'-lanterns or mechanical chickens, and even a brand-new haunted house. But what he was looking forward to more than anything was the corn maze that he remembered so well from four years ago.

He passed a multitude of other children, who walked around in wonderment similar to him, but most of them had strained looks on their faces, and when Tommy got the measure of the parents walking around, he knew what the problem was: all the parents seemed to be irritated, or downright angry. They were very short with their kids, not allowing them to do half the things they wanted, even though there was no good reason not to. It sounded like his father, and he sympathized. But he was with his sister today, and he didn't have to worry about any of that. Remembering this, he smiled and skipped on.

Tommy hopped along the trail toward the tractor that picked people up and gave them hayrides.

"Don't go too far!" Carmen called from somewhere behind him.

He turned and waved at her, slowing down a bit, but still continuing on.

Carmen watched him, noting that he was going for the tractor, then she ducked into an old shed that was for staff only. But she made sure the coast was clear and looked around the storage shed for something she could use. She picked up some trowels and shovels and tilling claws, getting a feel for each of them, but she didn't think any of them were made from iron. She moved on.

Tommy crossed a row of jack-o'-lanterns carved and displayed on a hill next to him. They all leered at him with their scary faces, and he felt a little nervous looking at them for some reason.

Just behind the hill, gliding by in the distance, he swore he saw a black, pointy hat.

Tommy stopped and stared.

The jack-o'-lanterns stared back.

He gulped and carried on. The path ahead of him branched off either toward the hayride or the corn maze. For some reason, an insidious touch of fear had been put into him, and he decided to go and do the maze first; he remembered he always felt safe there as a kid, neatly tucked within the rows of tall corn, where no one could get to him.

Carmen left the shed and walked down the path, looking toward the hayride. She didn't see Tommy standing in the crowd waiting for the tractor to pull up, and she spun around, searching for him. "Tommy?" she called. Then she glanced at the entrance to the corn maze and saw him slip inside. *There he is*, she thought.

She walked past a row of jack-o'-lanterns, giving them a quick glance on her way, and then one winked at her. She stopped.

THE WITCH OF HALLOWEEN HOUSE

There had been a projector set up to display moving faces on the un-carved pumpkins, but when Carmen looked closer at it, she saw that the projector wasn't on yet, because it was still daytime. The pumpkin definitely had a face carved into it, and it moved. Now the entire pumpkin shimmied to the edge of the bale of hay for her, its mouth widening as its jagged teeth grew into longer, sharper points before her very eyes.

"What the..." she muttered. Soon all of the pumpkins in the row came to life, and she heard a scream from behind her.

A large animatronic creature made out to look like a dinosaur composed of large pumpkins came to life and tore down a chain-link fence, lurching forward for a frightened little girl.

Carmen spun around and saw black robes gliding through the pumpkin patch in the field next to the corn maze. The witch raised her wand and suddenly all the pumpkins came to life, frightening visages being carved into them in real-time. Then the witch pointed her wand up at the sky and the sun plunged over the horizon like a bowling ball, bringing in a swift night.

A bitter chill swept over the farm, and Carmen turned to the corn maze, breathless. "Tommy!"

— CHAPTER TWENTY —

ROUNDED UP

The scene at the pumpkin patch turned to chaos as everyone scrambled, trying to get out of there. Every jack-o'-lantern in the place came alive, hopping or rolling around and snapping their jagged teeth, trying to ensnare the children. A fire started in the large pumpkin patch in the field next to the corn maze, and the blaze flashed quickly, forming a huge lasso sigil.

Parents scrambled in fear, some of them trying to collect their kids and escape, and others just outright abandoning their children and fending for themselves. Jack-o'-lanterns caught some of the young by the ankles, tripping them and dragging them away as their tiny fingers futilely clawed through the dirt.

Carmen dashed for the corn maze, clutching the witch mirror in her hand. She had to find her brother at all costs; she couldn't let the witch take him.

Tommy stumbled through the maze, he'd already made a number of turns and was already lost. He stared up at the sky fearfully, not able to understand why it had gotten dark already. He heard the screams outside the maze, but with the tall rows of corn surrounding him, he couldn't see what was going on. But he knew it must have been the witch. He took off in a run, sailing around the curves and bends, passing other frightened people making their way through the maze.

Sometimes he felt a looming shadow behind him, and he glanced over his shoulder, only to see the tall stalks of corn bending over him lifelessly.

Tall spotlights towered over the edges of the corn maze, illuminating the inside at night, and his hot breath came out as a white puff in the air. Tommy stared behind himself as he ran, sure that he felt a presence following him. He would periodically glance forward again to see where he was going before returning his gaze over his shoulder. He made a left turn, and then a right, then he glanced forward again.

The witch stood in front of him.

Tommy screeched to a halt, the heels of his shoes digging into the dirt. They slipped out from under him and he fell to his knees, scrambling to get up and retreat the other way. The witch followed, and it seemed no matter how many twists and turns Tommy took, she was right on his heels. He came to a dead-end in the maze and turned to see the witch gliding toward him, her wand raised.

Frantically, he dove for the dense corn, trying to pull it apart and climb through. A flash of green light struck the corn behind him, creating a splash of sparks and causing a few of the stalks to sag down at the knuckles.

It was very dark underneath the corn, and Tommy couldn't see where he was going. His heart rattled in his chest. He was operating on pure instinct. And his instinct told him that if he kept trying to go around the intended paths of the corn maze, he would never find his way out.

Carmen searched around the corn, shouting his name. She held the witch mirror up in front of her, as if she expected the witch to glide around a corner at any moment for her. She still didn't know exactly what it did, but Peter said it would protect her, and right now she clutched onto it for dear life.

"Tommy!" Carmen screamed. But she heard nothing. She narrowed her eyes as she ran, trying to find some kind of clue as to his whereabouts. Then she spotted something and stopped. She turned and saw some strangely-damaged cornstalks that were leaning over into the path. Some more cornstalks next to them were stretched apart, as if someone had tunneled through. And the makeshift tunnel was small.

Tommy dove into another patch of corn, worming his way through. His arms and shoulders were tired, as were his legs. His breath ran ragged in and out of his lungs, but he couldn't stop, not with the witch behind him. He glanced over his shoulder and watched the witch shift through the thick width of cornstalks he just crawled through. She shrieked and another streak of green light shot from the end of her wand. Tommy ducked and popcorn exploded from the stalks where it struck. He frantically dove into another thick width of corn and dug through it as fast as he could. When he got to the other side, he tumbled down a grassy hill and came to rest down in a little ditch.

When he got to his feet, he brushed himself off and saw that he had exited the corn maze in the farm. A stretch of woods sat ahead of him and he had no choice but to run for it as he saw the witch glide through the edge of the maze and pursue him.

He climbed as quickly as he could over the uneven ground, his legs fatigued now. More jets of green shot by, striking trees and peeling off the bark. Tommy ran for the whole quarter-mile that the woods lasted as the witch closed in. Then he spotted a road up ahead. It was dark, and he didn't think anyone would be around to help him, but screamed in his head for someone to save him. He exited the woods and ran at the steep bank of grass heading up to the road when another green bolt caught his ankle and tripped him. He fell to the ground and spun around, seeing the witch twenty yards away and closing in.

The thin green cord extended from the tip of the witch's wand and wrapped around his ankle, ensnaring him. The witch held him in place as her terrifying figure got closer and closer.

A flash of headlights shone down the lonely road behind Tommy, and he threw a glance at it. He looked at the magical cord and saw that it was looped over the tongue of his shoe and around the back of it.

Summoning a burst of courage, Tommy quickly untied his shoelace to loosen it, then he shimmied his foot out of it. The witch's lasso snapped shut and was pulled back into her wand like a roll of measuring tape.

Tommy got up and ran up to the road, yelling and waving his arms.

The horn blared and the car swerved to a stop next to him.

He ran up to the passenger doors, banging on the windows and screaming for the driver to let him in.

The passenger window rolled down and a man leaned past a girl sitting in the seat next to him and said, "Get in, little dude."

Tommy pulled open the door in the back and climbed in, yelling for the driver to get them out of there.

"Tommy?" a familiar voice said.

He looked over and saw Brett sitting next to him, then he realized that it was Stacy sitting in the passenger seat with her boyfriend Vince driving.

Vince didn't seem to take his warning seriously, and he slowly put the car back in drive and eased onto the accelerator. But the car cruised down the dark road, and Tommy pressed his face to the window, not seeing the witch chasing them. The radio was off, and no one talked after Tommy had calmed down, creating an eerie silence.

"What happened to you?" Brett said.

"The witch came after me!" Tommy replied. "In the corn maze!"

Brett's eyes widened. "We saw her too. She came after me and the other guys, and we got split up after some bats attacked us. Man, things are going crazy around here."

"Don't talk about witches!" Stacy said sharply from the front seat. "That's ridiculous."

Brett rolled his eyes and looked at Tommy. "*She doesn't believe me,*" he whispered. "*But I see what's going on. I see all the kids being taken...*"

"I know where she's taking them!" Tommy said.

"Where?"

"To the church!"

Vince looked in the rearview mirror. "To the church it is, little buddy," he said in a robotic voice. He sank his foot on the gas pedal and the car picked up speed.

Stacy shoved him in the shoulder. "What the hell, Vince? We're not going to the church! I need to get Brett back home."

But Vince wouldn't listen. A turn came up on the left, and Vince took it, heading for the church at the edge of town.

Tommy gulped. He wasn't equipped to go there right now. He just wanted to get out of here and find his sister; Vince didn't know what he was getting them into.

"I'm serious, Vince!" Stacy cried. "Turn around!"

He ignored her.

"If you won't turn around, then stop this car right now! Me and Brett are getting out and walking!"

Vince pulled the car to an abrupt stop, and Tommy and Brett were thrown into the seats in front of them. Stacy pushed open the passenger door. "Come on, Brett," she said, stepping out into the cold night.

As soon as she was out of the car, Vince stepped on the accelerator again and the vehicle shot forward without her. Tommy and Brett spun around in their seats and watched Stacy scream and flail her arms in the middle of the road behind them, yelling for Vince to stop.

Vince reached over and adjusted the rearview mirror, staring at the two of them with cold eyes. "All the kids like going to the church," he said. "They all love the church, yes they do." The way he delivered his sentences was monotonous and very inhuman. It sent a chill down the kids' spines, and as Tommy watched him, he saw the exact mannerisms that his father had exhibited lately.

Carmen came out of the woods toward the road. "Tommy!" she screamed, looking around. Then she saw something a few paces from her. She ran over and picked it up, and her heart plunged to her toes.

It was Tommy's shoe.

Tears flowed down her face, and she knew that he'd been taken by the witch to the church. She wasn't ready to go there yet, but she didn't have any more time. It was now or never if she ever wanted to see her brother alive again.

— CHAPTER TWENTY-ONE —

INTO THE WITCH'S SNARE

Vince's Pontiac crawled up the hill and its headlights flashed across the parking lot. It slowly rolled to the other end and stopped in front of the church. The headlights washed against the welcome sign sitting at the start of the path leading up to the church doors.

Tommy and Brett sat nervously in the back of the car, and they waited in silence for Vince to say something, but he just sat there.

"Can we go?" Tommy asked.

"Yes," Vince said, "into the church." He stared at the two of them in his rearview mirror.

"I meant go home," Tommy said quietly.

But Vince just sat there, his steely eyes staring at them through the rearview mirror.

"Come on Vince, this isn't funny," Brett said. "I don't want to be here."

"Go in the church," Vince said emotionlessly.

"No way," Brett said, holding his arms across his chest.

Vince put the car into park, then he opened his door and stepped out. Brett watched in fear as he walked to the back and opened his door. When Vince reached in and grabbed him by the collar, Brett put his hands up defensively.

"Okay, okay!" he said. He got out of the car and backed away from Vince, and Tommy did the same, not wanting to be near the man alone.

Without another word, Vince got back in the driver's seat and turned the car around, speeding out of view down the hill.

The two boys found themselves in the empty parking lot of the church that was about as far on the outskirts of town as they could get. The church itself was Irish Catholic, and it sat at the edge of a cliff overlooking a river flowing down below. It was normally a picturesque place to visit, but as the two boys turned around and saw the building standing against the dimness of the moonlight, their skin crawled.

"This is where the witch has been taking them?" Brett asked.

"Yeah," Tommy replied. "Me and my sister found some clues that led here." He looked around and saw the little marsh in the distance near the start of the long and winding roads leading up to the church's parking lot where the timothy-grass grew. Then he turned and looked at the gardens on the west side of the building and saw the same flowers that had been in the box, and one or two of the weeds.

"So are they... inside?" Brett asked. There didn't appear to be any activity outside, nor inside for that matter, as all the lights in the church were off. Beautiful stained-glass windows adorned the east and west sides of the building, but any visible glow coming through them was absent.

Brett turned and looked down the road, thinking about Vince. "I really hate him, you know," he said suddenly.

Tommy turned to him. "He seems the same as my dad," he said. "I think he's being controlled."

Brett dismissed him. "He was like that before all this started. He reminds me a lot of my dad before he left." Brett had always kept up a tough shell, keeping anyone from getting too close to him, and Tommy could finally see where he got it from.

"Does he always hit you?" Tommy asked.

Brett stared out at the edge of the cliff past the church. "You know, let's just go, okay?" There was irritation in his voice, and Tommy knew it must have been a tender subject. "It can't take that long to walk home from here, could it?" Brett asked.

"But what about all the kids that disappeared?" Tommy asked, turning back to the church.

"I really don't want to go in there," Brett said, and his apprehension was surprising to Tommy; normally Brett would be the first one to sneak into a place at night.

"Well I'm going in," Tommy said. He was terrified of what he would find, but all the clues seemed to lead to here, and if he could help save someone, he would; it's what his mother always taught him was right when she was still around, and his father even taught him the same lesson back when he spent more time parenting and less time working.

Tommy walked along the pathway and came up to the tall and wide doors at the front of the church. Brett was left in the lurch behind him, but he could only take standing in the darkness by himself for so long before he grunted and joined him.

They pulled on the doors, expecting them to be locked, but they swung open easily, as if someone was expecting them. They found themselves in a small coat room, and there was a doorway beyond that led to a lobby. All of the lights were out, and it didn't look like anyone was inside.

"Are you sure you got the right spot?" Brett asked.

Tommy's eyes scrunched up. "I think so," he said. He moved forward carefully and spotted a light switch on the wall as the door to the church he'd opened slowly swung closed behind them. He flicked it on and to his delight the lobby lit up with white fluorescents. They crossed into the sanctuary, which they could barely see from the off-glow of the lights in the lobby, but it seemed empty, too.

Their footsteps echoed in the large room as they plodded across the carpet. Brett found the light switch and turned it on, and half of the lights in the sanctuary illuminated over their heads. The boys searched the large room, but there was no one there; no children; no witches.

Tommy's fear was starting to settle down, and he became confused. Could he have been wrong about this place? If the witch wasn't keeping all the children here, then where?

"Doesn't this place have a basement?" Brett asked suddenly, remembering a time many years ago when his aunt had forced him to come here with the family.

Suddenly Tommy remembered this too. His father and mother had taken him and his sister to church four years ago, not long before she died. They never came much before, but his mom wanted to leave a lasting impression of tradition and family on his young, impressionable mind. Sadly, that lesson had certainly fallen through the cracks. But when they took him and his sister here, they would sometimes run downstairs in the basement and play.

Tommy and Brett walked to opposite ends of the sanctuary and searched around the pews at the front. Tommy opened a door to a small room next to the stage and pulled dusty white cloths off of old furniture.

When he returned, Brett stood on the far side of the large room, facing one of the stained-glass windows. His head was pointed down to the carpet and it looked like he was shaking. When Tommy called his name, Brett quickly wiped an arm across his face, then he turned around, but kept his face pointed away from Tommy.

"What do you want?" Brett asked.

Tommy walked up to him. "Are you okay?"

"I'm fine," he said. "Get away from me!" Brett shoved him and Tommy stumbled to a pew, falling hard on the wooden seat.

Brett marched up onto the stage as if nothing happened, and he noticed a display sitting at the back. He walked up to it and peered down at the glass case. "Cool!" he said.

Tommy was confused at what he saw from Brett, and his sudden change in demeanor, but he got up cautiously and joined him on the stage. "What is it?"

"It's a knife or something. Maybe a dagger."

"A ceremonial knife, maybe?" Tommy suggested, admiring the way the curved blade attached to the hilt, and the decorations etched into it.

"Get it for me," Brett said.

"What?"

"Break the glass and take it," Brett said. "I want it."

Tommy shook his head. "No."

Brett shoved him again. "What's your problem? Don't you want to hang out with me? I didn't know you were such a dumb ass."

"I don't want to steal it," Tommy said. "That's wrong."

Before Tommy could give another excuse, Brett tipped over the display's stand and it crashed open on the floor, shattering to pieces. Brett bent down and picked up the dagger, eyeing it proudly and feeling the weight of it in his hand.

"What are you doing, Brett?" Tommy asked.

"I'm taking this, what's it look like?"

"No, I mean why are you acting like this? Bullying me? It isn't right. I saw Vince bully you, and you didn't look like you liked it very much. So why are you doing it to me?" Tommy's nature was inquisitive and honest, and it was like Brett's kryptonite when confronted with it.

Brett's face faltered. His mouth fell open and he tried to say something, but when he couldn't find the words to directly face his problems, anger rose in him instead. He gripped the blade of the knife tighter as his face went red. "I... You..."

Tommy saw the knife in his hand and backed up slowly. "We don't have to fight," he said quickly. "I thought we were friends?"

A tear dropped out of Brett's eye, and his face twisted into horror when he felt it stream down his cheek. He dropped the knife and took off running, wiping his face with his sleeve.

"Wait!" Tommy cried and chased after him.

Brett took a left out of the sanctuary and headed for the staircase going down to the basement. Tommy followed him to the stairs and watched as he fled down into the darkness. He stopped suddenly, not wanting to run headlong into the unknown. "Brett!" he called. But he didn't answer.

Tommy didn't want to go down there, but he couldn't just leave Brett alone like that, especially if there was something down there that neither one of them wanted to see. Tommy held the railing tightly and slowly made his way down. He called out Brett's name a few times, listening as the silence answered him.

His feet touched the basement floor, and he felt the coldness wash over the area. Tommy fumbled around in the dark for a light switch, and as his finger touched it, his heart seized, afraid of what horrors waited for him when he shone a light upon them.

The bulb flickered on over his head, casting the area in a pale glow. The main section of the basement was empty, and there were a few rooms connected to it. Some were for storage, one was a play area for the kids, and one was a library. Distant memories came back to him as Tommy crept around in the dark, poking his head in each room.

"Brett?" he said.

Sobbing came from behind him.

Tommy turned around slowly, staring back across the basement. There was one last storage room that he hadn't checked yet. He made his way over to it. His fingers slid along the dark wall inside, then he turned on the light. Stacks of boxes sat in the middle of the room with furniture pushed around the edges. The soft sobs came from the other side of the boxes.

Tommy's heart beat rapidly. "Brett?" He walked around to the other side and saw Brett's miserable shape curled up on the floor with his knees hiked to his chest. His head snapped up at him and he saw a mess of red and wet eyes. Brett held an arm over his face to shield the shame.

"Go away!" Brett said.

Tommy was dumbfounded; he had never seen Brett this... this *vulnerable*.

"I can't do it anymore!" Brett sobbed. "It's all my fault!"

"What's your fault?" Tommy asked.

"Everything!" he said. "All of this! If it wasn't for me, no one would be hurt or missing. Nobody would be acting weird!"

"What are you talking about?"

"I did it! *Okay?*" he cried, offering his hands up in appeasement. "I burned down Halloween House with the witch inside!"

"You *what?*" Tommy asked, shocked.

"I didn't mean to! Everyone was standing around her house, throwing rocks and stuff. I thought it looked fun, so when no one was looking, I snuck around to the back and lit a fire. It was just supposed to be a joke! I thought someone would put it out! I didn't mean to do all that!" He sank his head in his hands and started bawling, his chest heaving up and down with miserable sobs.

Tommy walked up to him and cautiously placed his hand on Brett's back.

"Get off me!" Brett shouted, knocking his hand away.

Tommy took a step back. "It's okay, it's not your fault. You didn't know."

Brett looked up and considered him for a moment, then he turned his head away again and stared at the floor.

Tommy turned around, feeling cold from the startling revelation. Then he thought again about everything that had happened since, including the witch supposedly kidnapping the children and bringing them to the church. But they had been upstairs in the church and now he had seen every room in the basement, but the entire place was empty; there were no kids anywhere. Had he been wrong about this place?

"Now things will never be the same again," Brett muttered, starting to calm down. "I just wanna—" Brett paused in midsentence, reaching behind him and plucking something off the back of his neck. He held the strange item in front of him and looked at it. "What the hell, Tommy? Why did you throw this at me?" He held it out to him, and Tommy saw that it was a flower from the garden outside the church.

"I didn't," Tommy said.

Brett reached behind his neck again and pulled out something else stuck to his coat. He looked at the timothy-grass and then threw it on the ground, smacking the back of his neck repeatedly with his hands to get it all off. He turned to Tommy to ask how it all got there, and then he noticed something on the floor. "What the...?"

Tommy turned to the doorway.

Weeds and flowers—all the clues that had led Tommy here in the first place—lined the floor in a trail leading out the door of the room.

Brett stood up and the two of them silently drifted out of the room into the main section of the basement.

The trail let up the stairs the way they'd come, and they both stared at it, questions filling their minds. They rounded the corner and came up onto the ground floor, and then they both gasped.

Lining the lobby were hundreds of lengths of rope, with a loop tied on the end like a lasso. Well over a two hundred of them were strewn all across the floor like hungry snakes, and many dozens were hanging from the ceiling like nooses.

Tommy suddenly realized it was a mistake to want to come here in the first place. And as the lights flickered and the witch appeared in the room in front of them, he realized that the church was never a place where the witch kept the children; it was only a trap.

--- --- ---

Carmen ran across the parking lot to the front doors of the church, her lungs burning. She heard screams inside, and she opened one of the doors just in time to see Tommy cowering in the far corner of the lobby as the witch slowly glided to him. Brett was knocked out, lying face-first on the floor. She looked up momentarily, mesmerized by all of the ropes, terrified at what was going on.

"Tommy!" she screamed.

"Help!" Tommy cried from the corner as the witch closed in.

Carmen took a step in the doorway and pulled out her witch mirror that she hung around her neck. She held it up and tried to do something with it, but in the next moment she found herself sailing through the air, something like a sonic wave hitting her and sending her flying. She crashed onto the cement sidewalk and grunted from the dull pain. The door to the church slammed shut, and when she got back to her feet, yelling her brother's name and pounding on the door, she found that it was firmly locked.

She took a step back and watched as swirling black energy seemed to emanate inside the church, visible through the stained-glass windows.

"Tommy!" she cried. She wrenched on the doors, but they wouldn't open. She picked up a rock and threw it at one of the windows, but it bounced off, and it would have been too high up for her to climb through, anyway.

She heard a final shriek from her brother, and then like a star collapsing and sucking in on itself, the sounds of the swirling energy shrunk to a central point, and then there was only silence.

Carmen tried the doors again, and this time they opened. There were no more ropes in the empty lobby. And Tommy and Brett were gone.

She started crying, as her face twisted into a horrid mess of emotion and guilt. The thought of losing her brother to the witch was overwhelming, and she couldn't believe she had let that happen. She cried his name, as if it would help, and she ran through the entire church, desperately searching for him. But after going through the basement and ending in the sanctuary, she was left alone. She climbed onto the stage at the front of the sanctuary and saw broken glass strewn across the floor.

There was an item amidst the glass, and she bent to pick it up. It was a strange curved dagger. There was a yellowed sheet of paper amidst the glass and she held it up to find that it was a historical description of the dagger. It was an old Irish blade that men used to carry, and her eyes flicked through the paper line by line until they fell on the word "iron".

Carmen paused, deep in thought. She wiped the tears out of her eyes. So she had the salt, she had the garlic, and now she had an iron knife and a witch mirror to protect herself. But what could she do with all of it? Where was the witch hiding, anyway? Where were the children?

The more she thought about it, the more she came to one singular conclusion. She thought of her dad delivering the strange box. She and her brother hadn't seen anything there, but they must have missed something; everything had to be at Halloween House. If her brother was still alive, then he was there; she could feel it, and she would do anything, even giving her own life, to get him back.

— CHAPTER TWENTY-TWO —

BRAWL

Carmen ripped open the door to the police station and hurried through it. Some officers standing around turned their heads to her, but she didn't give them any attention as she made her way to the jail cells at the back. She didn't even look into her father's office; she was only here for one reason.

The officer sitting at the desk in the booking area of the cells glanced up, seeing a blur of motion in his periphery, but she was already gone before he could see her.

Carmen went to the end and peered into Peter's jail cell, only to find it empty. She frantically looked in the other cells, but she didn't see him. "No..." she said. She turned around and stormed for her father's office.

He was sitting inside with his feet up on the desk. He stared blankly at the wall next to the door, and when she walked in, his eyes lazily dragged over to her. He seemed completely gone now, like he was a shell of his former self. His eyes scrunched up suddenly and he rubbed the back of his neck.

"Hi there, Sweetpea," he said. But none of the love and warmth was in it anymore.

"Where is he?" she demanded.

"I think it's past your bedtime," he said. "Let me drive you home and tuck you in."

"*Where's Peter?*"

But he just blankly stared at her.

She knew that she would get nowhere with him; he was too far gone. Everyone was too far gone. Suddenly she felt foolish for thinking that she could affect any of this at all. She was overwhelmed by it, by how everything had seemed normal just a few days ago, and now her whole world was a mess. She threw herself onto his desk and cried.

Robert took his feet off the surface and leaned forward, patting her on the back in a pseudo-human gesture.

But Carmen viciously threw him off, grimacing and standing up. "Don't do that!" she said. Whatever this thing was in front of her, it wasn't her father, and it had no business pretending to be.

"Where are they?!" Carmen shrieked. "Where are the children?! Where's Tommy?!" She slammed her fists down on his desk. "What have you done to them?!" She started bawling, and her hand fell on her chest inside her open coat.

There was a dull warmth under her palm, and she looked down to see the witch mirror hanging around her neck, the smooth stone of it slipped inside her shirt. She pulled it out and saw that the stone was glowing, just like it had the night the witch chased them into the house and Robert had shown up, acting strangely.

Carmen looked up and saw her father's eyes wide, staring at the stone. She glanced back down at it, drawing a connection. She held the stone up in the air from around her neck, closer to him, and he backed up in his chair.

She glanced over her shoulder at the hallway behind her, then she quietly shut the door and locked it.

Robert stood up cautiously, taking a few steps back into the corner.

She stepped around one side of the desk, and he matched her movements on the other side. "You don't like this, do you?" she asked the thing in front of her.

Robert pressed his back to the corner of the room as Carmen whipped around, then he pushed himself out and tried to get out of the door, fumbling with the lock. But Carmen came up behind him and pressed the stone to the back of his neck. He shrieked and elbowed her in the neck. Carmen stumbled back onto the desk as Robert howled in pain, a searing burn etched into his flesh. He turned for the door again, and Carmen took the necklace off of her, setting back in on him. He opened the door, but she managed to jump up and wrap her arms around his neck, pulling him backward. They both crashed into the desk, and Carmen held the stone onto his skin.

It was like a hot iron to him and he cried in pain, bucking her off and stumbling onto his hands and knees on the floor. He got up to his feet quickly, then he doubled over suddenly, shaking his head like a wild animal. His face twisted into a litany of emotions, and he rubbed the back of his neck hard, like he was trying to get an itch he couldn't scratch. He started grunting and coughing, and the voice that did so seemed much closer to her father than the one she'd known in the last couple days. He continued to struggle with himself and he strode quickly out of the room, his lips pulled back into a grimace and his eyes strained shut.

Carmen lay on the desk, staring at him. She heard him go to the back of the station, and then she heard a door open. She picked herself up and looked into the hallway.

Some other officers were standing around, staring at her and down the hall where Robert had gone, but they didn't seem to be too concerned.

Carmen composed herself, clutching the witch mirror in her hand, then she casually made her way out the back door of the station into the alley next to the vehicle pool. "Dad?" she asked timidly. She looked around but didn't see him. Then she heard the flicking of a lighter around the corner. She walked around the building to see him standing in another alley on the opposite side from the vehicle pool. Her father was leaning against the wall, his collar pulled loose, and a cigarette hung from his lips.

"Dad?" she said again.

His hands were shaking as he tried to light the cigarette. Catching the flame to the end of it, he took a long drag, then removed it from his mouth and exhaled. Cool smoke blew out and intermingled with the night air. He glanced over at her, and the eyes were familiar. She didn't know if he was quite all there, but she saw flashes of her father—her real father.

"Dad, you don't smoke anymore..." She took a step toward him, but he held out his hand.

"Get away!" he said.

"But Dad..."

His face scrunched up suddenly and he pressed his hand to his forehead, like he was trying to wipe something off. His teeth ground together, and he grunted. "Just stay away from me," he warned. "I'm not... I'm not safe."

"Let me help you," she said, holding out the witch mirror to him.

His eyes widened in horror. "No! Please... no more!" He took another drag of the cigarette and let it out, then he looked down at the wedding band on his finger, and she saw something like reverie in his eyes.

"You're thinking about Mom, aren't you?" she said. "You're still there, Dad. I can see you under all of this."

His face scrunched up again like he was in horrible agony. "I can't fight it!" he said in a strained voice. "It's coming back over me!"

"Just don't be afraid," she said. "Don't give into the fear!"

He shook his head violently, throwing the cigarette against the wall in a rage. "It's too late for that." His head snapped up suddenly and he looked at her with sober eyes, like it was the last chance he had to say something genuine to her. "They're at the house," he said. "They're all at the house. I can see them."

"Tommy's there?" she asked. "Can you help me?"

He shook his head violently, then he scratched his throat. "Take my cruiser and go." He pulled the keys out of his pocket and tossed them at her. "You're the only one who can."

And with that, he doubled over and dry-retched, furiously rubbing the back of his neck. Then a wave seemed to pass over him, calming him down. He stood up again, and his eyes glazed over. He looked at her.

"Why don't I take you home, Sweetpea?" he said.

Carmen looked down at the witch mirror in her hand and then her father, considering it, but she knew it would probably cause him excruciating pain, and it wouldn't be enough to save him. There was only one thing that could: stopping the witch.

Carmen left her father in the alley as he blankly stared at her and watched her go. She came out onto the street and saw the front door to the police station open. Stacy came out, stopping and turning in the door.

"What is *wrong* with you?!" she shrieked toward the officers. "Why won't you help me find my brother?!" She gave a frustrated grunt and she turned away, finding Carmen right in front of her. She paused like a deer in the headlights, then she rushed over to her. "Where the hell is my brother?" she asked. "You have to know where he is, don't you? Where did that little twerp of yours take him?"

"I saw them at the church!" Carmen said. "But the witch... she took them."

Stacy's eyes widened. "What? You saw Brett? Why didn't you take him out of there?!"

"It was too late by the time I got there," Carmen said. "They're both gone. Gone to the house up in the woods."

"Why did you let her take him?!" Stacy screamed, shoving her.

Carmen stumbled back. This was the last thing she needed. "Don't touch me," she said.

But Stacy had already flown into a rage. She came at her again and shoved her, then she started into a tirade, scratching at her face furiously.

Carmen reeled back and shoved Stacy away from her, her own lips stretched back into a scowl. Since Tommy had been taken, she'd been trying to control her fear, but that control was slipping away now. She felt a deep anger born inside of her, growing and flooding through her whole body. When she looked at Stacy, she saw a big red and white target painted on her, and her hands curled into claws.

Carmen launched herself forward and fought back against Stacy. The two of them locked into a catfight that was quickly taken to the ground. Stacy slashed her face, cutting her cheek, then Carmen flipped her over and straddled her, thrashing her with fingernails and fists. A strong punch connected with Stacy's jaw and her head was rattled. She landed another one, and another one as Stacy was knocked silly. With one more punch, she was out cold, then Carmen sat upright, horror dawning on her.

What had she done?

Carmen got off of her, and stayed on her knees, rolling Stacy's jaw with her hand. But she was out like a light. Carmen stood up, her legs weak. Her arms shook, and her fists felt numb. She would never ever do something like this, not even in the face of Stacy's attacks and belittlement, and she felt a strange sensation swim through her head. It urged her to do more; to find someone else and fight them, too. A part of her wanted to tear the whole town apart, but her mind—that good, wholesome part of her mind that had been nurtured and brought up by her mother—furiously fought against it. She took a step back in horror and looked around. She had to go save Tommy, but she couldn't leave Stacy here like this.

She bent down and hooked Stacy under the armpits, then she dragged her around the station to the vehicle pool. She set her down gently next to her father's cruiser, then unlocked it with the keys he'd given her. She opened the back door and struggled under Stacy's weight to carry her inside. When she was laid out across the back, she shut the door and climbed in the driver's seat. Sliding the keys into the ignition and turning the engine over, she did a quick inventory. She had the salt, the garlic, and the knife in her coat pockets. She had the witch mirror, too, and there was nothing else to do but to be brave and drive up to Halloween House. She turned the flashing lights on like she'd seen her father do a million times, then she pulled out of the parking lot and sped into the night for the house, praying that she got there before it was too late.

— CHAPTER TWENTY-THREE —

Crossing the Gauntlet

She sped through the streets of the small town, heading for the edge of the woods. No children were out trick-or-treating, and in fact, barely anyone was out at all. A few cars passed by her, their drivers not appearing to care that a police cruiser was going by with its sirens on. Carmen glanced over her shoulder periodically at Stacy lying in the back, but she was still out cold. When she got to the woods, she slowed down and took the car off road.

The frame of the car bumped and heaved over the uneven ground, then she hit the long incline toward the house. She slowed right down, maneuvering around the trees like a slalom race. Her dad had let her drive his cruiser around a little bit in parking lots before, and down the street just once, but she didn't even have her license, so it was difficult for her to get around the trees without crashing into anything. The car lurched over a large mound and the front of the bumper slammed into the ground, shooting up a plume of dirt. She hit the brake as Stacy's body rolled into the back of her seat.

She went slowly and carefully, getting farther up the hill. The trees became denser, and at a certain point, she wondered if it would be faster just to get out and go on foot. Finally a line of trees came up ahead and she couldn't see a way through them. She pulled the cruiser to a stop and looked around for an alternate route, but she didn't see one. She stared up the hill, but the house still wasn't quite in sight yet.

Stacy groaned in the backseat.

Carmen killed the ignition and got out of the car. She opened up Stacy's door and Stacy looked up at her, rubbing her jaw.

"What happened?" she asked.

"Sorry about that," Carmen said, offering her a hand.

But Stacy looked at her suspiciously. She sat up on her own, glancing around, then she got scared. "Where are we?"

"I brought us up to Halloween House," Carmen said. "To the witch."

"Why do you keep talking about a witch?" Stacy demanded. "The only witch I see here is you."

Carmen felt the sting of anger rising in her again, but she took a step back and drew in a deep breath, letting Stacy climb out of the cruiser. "Your brother's somewhere up in that house," she said, pointing. "So is mine, and I'm going in there to get him."

"Brett's up there?" she said, turning her head. "Brett!" she shouted, then she took off running up the hill.

"Wait!" Carmen called after her. "It's dangerous!" She turned back to the cruiser, making sure she had everything she brought. She pulled a flashlight out of the car that her father kept there, then she turned and followed Stacy.

The night was bitterly cold and the wind howled over top of them. Bare tree branches moved slightly in the wind, giving an eerie life to the woods.

A light glowed ahead.

Stacy saw this. "Brett? Are you there?" She ran up the hill, and Carmen struggled to keep up with her.

"Stacy! Wait a minute!"

Carmen saw her stop up ahead, and when she caught up to her, she saw that there was a long line of jack-o'-lanterns curving up a path toward the house. The blackened husk sat in the distance beyond them at the top of the hill, and their faces glowed as flickering orange flames danced inside each one.

Stacy looked at them for a moment, then she turned away and carried on up the hill for the house.

"Stacy, watch out!" Carmen said.

The jack-o'-lanterns started to move, their carved faces shifting like they were alive. Then a cold wind swept across the floor of the woods, raking up all the leaves and twigs and dirt together in a small whirlwind. The debris clustered up to the edges of the pumpkins, and then the jack-o'-lanterns rose into the air as pillars of nature packed themselves together underneath them, forming humanoid bodies. An army of jack-o'-lanterns turned to them and their grins widened, their orange teeth sharp.

Stacy screamed. "Oh my God! What the hell are these things?!" She took off running to the side, trying to get away from them.

Carmen looked around for a weapon and spotted a big branch that had snapped off a tree. She picked it up and brandished it at the gruesome creatures as they came for her. Carmen skirted around to the side as well, swinging the stick at them to keep them at bay.

Leaves and dirt shook off of them as they moved, and they lumbered slowly toward her. She smacked one with the branch, and a large section of its body was knocked away, causing the pumpkin to tumble off and smash on the ground. Another one took a swing at her with its long arm of packed dirt and stones. The arm exploded across Carmen's cheek, rocking her head back and making her stumble. Dirt and debris flew everywhere in a shower as the armless man continued for her. Hard stones had been packed in the dirt, causing incredible pain in her jaw.

Stacy shrieked up ahead as a jack-o'-lantern grabbed her and sank its teeth into her leg. The pumpkin's teeth had hardened like stone, and they cut through her skin easily. She spun around onto her back and kicked at it. It held strong at first, but as she furiously rained kicks on it, the top of its head caved in and turned into a goopy mess, then its body disintegrated all at once into a man-shaped pile on the ground. Stacy got up as more pumpkin-men approached, and she fled up to the house.

Carmen came up the rear, swinging the branch wildly at them. She knocked a few of them apart, and the jack-o'-lanterns that fell to the ground but hadn't smashed, waited until more earth swirled and formed new bodies underneath them, then they stood and stalked her again.

She swung the branch hard down on one, and the branch snapped in half as the creature fell. She stomped on the jack-o'-lantern and smashed it to bits, then she swiveled her hips and drove a fist into the head of another one. She dented it, but she mostly just bruised her knuckles. Shaking her fist out in pain, another man came up behind her and wrapped its filthy hands around her throat, squeezing her. In desperation, Carmen turned and grabbed the jack-o'-lantern. It seemed to be fused onto the dirt-body by some kind of strange adhesion or force, but she ripped it off with all her might, and finally the head popped off the body and she hurled it at a tree, watching it smash and rain down soft innards and seeds everywhere.

She ran up the hill and saw Stacy ahead, realizing that the army of horrifying men were behind them, largely vanquished.

A cacophonous shriek filled the sky, one that was all too familiar to Carmen's ears.

"Oh no..." she muttered as she looked up. Stacy paused too and saw a strange cloud moving through the sky past the bare branches of the trees above them.

"What is that?" Stacy asked as Carmen caught up to her.

"We have to move!" Carmen shouted, pulling her along.

The cloud of bats swooped down and dove at them through the trees. Thankfully the trees were dense where they were, and most of them got caught up in the branches, even injuring themselves to try to get to them.

Carmen and Stacy crouched down, holding their arms above their heads to try to protect themselves. The bats flapped and nipped at them before swooping off to make another pass. The rodents curved through the air and dove again, and Carmen pulled the back of her coat over the top of her head to protect herself, but they still nipped at the knuckles on her exposed hands.

Stacy screamed as she fought them off, and she struggled to get up the hill. Carmen grabbed her arm and they both slowly made their way up as the bats flew off again.

The house sat up ahead, its dark husk faintly illuminated in the moonlight. They could already feel its presence now, especially strong now that it was Halloween night. It was ominous and brooding, and Carmen got a terrible feeling in the pit of her stomach. The answer to all the questions and fears sat in there, and her body screamed at her not to know them and turn away. But she wouldn't be stopped.

The bats dove down for one final pass, and they braced themselves. But when the flying mob neared the trees, the bats suddenly tilted upward and sailed back into the air, scattering apart and flying into the night.

Carmen and Stacy took a breath, watching them go. They took a moment to look at their injuries, which admittedly weren't too bad considering what they'd been through. Stacy's breath rattled out of her mouth, and soft tears came out of her eyes. She wiped them away, then she started forward again, looking at the house in fear. She walked a few paces, and then she stopped, staring down at her hands. She shrieked.

"What is it?" Carmen asked. She rushed up to her to see what was wrong, then she put a hand to her mouth.

Terrible boils had broken out over Stacy's skin, and Carmen could see them all over her hands and her face. Stacy scratched at them and one of them popped, oozing liquid over her chin.

"What is it?!" she cried. "What's happening to me?!"

Carmen looked down at her own skin and saw one form on the back of her hand. She felt the panic in her chest, then she took a deep breath and watched as the boil faded away. "Just stay calm," she told Stacy. "It's feeding off your fear! Don't be afraid, and it will go away."

"I... I can't!" she said, turning and stumbling for the house. "I have to get Brett!"

Carmen stopped and watched her go, unable to help her. The house was only a few dozen yards in front of them now, and Carmen could see its entire exterior, or what was left of it, clearly in the moonlight. Her heart lurched when Stacy disappeared into the house without a moment's thought, and then she was out of sight. She waited on pins and needles, not even noticing that she was holding her breath. The wind had stopped, and the hill was silent.

Then a bloodcurdling scream erupted from inside the house.

— CHAPTER TWENTY-FOUR —

SENTINEL

Carmen turned on the flashlight and clutched it in her cold hand as she stepped on the porch of the house. The horrible smell drifted out of it and filled her nostrils, and her body shook with fear. She told herself to calm down, but it was overwhelming standing here right now.

She found herself in the burned-out room that had been half-claimed by the fire. The wind swept by on the back of her injured neck, and she turned the beam of the flashlight across the blackened interior. The inside of the house was silent, and her eyes fell on the open doorway ahead, fearful of what lay beyond.

She crept forward slowly, listening to the floorboards creak under her. She rounded a pile of rubbish and stood in front of the doorway, shining the flashlight through.

Tommy stared at her.

Carmen was startled, and her breath caught in her throat. She wanted to cry out his name and rush forward to hug him, but there was something about his demeanor that was off-putting.

"Tommy?" she asked slowly.

He just stood and stared at her, and he had that same glazed-over look in his eyes as their father did.

"Welcome," he said.

"Tommy... where are the others? What happened to Stacy?"

"They're home now," he said. "They've all come home. You'll come home too."

Carmen's eyes flicked down to something held in Tommy's hand that was glinting in the light. "What are you holding?"

He moved his hand behind his leg so she couldn't see.

"What are you holding?" she repeated.

He walked toward her, and Carmen stumbled away from the doorway.

She watched him move, unnerved by the blank look on his face as he closed in, moving ever so slowly. Her heel caught on something and she crashed onto a blackened pile of garbage. Something hard struck her back and she cried out in pain. She looked up and saw Tommy's arm raised above his head, his face expressionless, as he plunged the shard of metal at her.

Carmen rolled out of the way and picked herself up on the other side of him. He approached again, backing her into the doorway. She kept the flashlight on him, but she kept glancing over her shoulder at the blackness behind her, fearful of what lurked within it.

"Tommy, don't do this," she said as she passed through the doorway. "Don't do this!"

"Come home, sister," he said, slipping through the doorway and following her through the darkness. He raised his arm again and held the twisted metal up for another slash.

Carmen waved the flashlight over her shoulder to see behind her, then she quickly returned it to her brother, fearful that he would lunge at her at any moment and plunge the metal into her flesh. She fumbled with her free hand to pull out the witch mirror hanging around her neck, holding up the stone at him. He didn't seem to be deterred, but he kept his eyes on it as he moved.

They played a delicate game as Carmen backed into the darkness. She held her witch mirror, and Tommy held his weapon. They were locked into a stalemate, neither one of them wanting to make the first move.

Carmen's shoulder bumped into a wall, and she spun the flashlight around to see where she was going. There was an open door next to her, leading into the kitchen, and she shifted over and backed into it.

When she turned the flashlight back on her brother, he was charging forward in a brisk walk and had already closed the distance. Carmen screamed as the metal came down, slashing her arm open. She stumbled backward and hit the old oven in the blackened kitchen. Her arm holding the flashlight was shaking, and her brother's moving figure glided through it at her again. In her panic, Carmen stumbled backward, forgetting that there was an open set of stairs behind her.

The ground was pulled out from under her and she tumbled down, hitting the stairs hard. A few of them snapped, while others held together, and she was thrust off the side of them, coming to rest on the basement floor.

She whimpered and weakly turned over as she watched her brother march down the stairs. He skipped over the ones that had broken like he was playing a game of hopscotch, then he rounded the bottom of them and faced her, holding his makeshift dagger up.

Carmen plucked up the witch mirror again from around her neck and held it up to him like a crucifix against the devil. He came for her and sank onto his knees, driving the metal at her face. She rolled out of the way and wrapped her arm around his neck, pulling him to her chest. He swung his arm around, trying to drive the metal into her, and she frantically rolled out of the way to avoid it. She drove his back against the ground and pinned his wrist to the floor, then she took the glowing rose-colored stone of the witch mirror and pressed it to his neck as she hugged him.

Tommy screamed as his flesh seared.

"I'm sorry! I'm sorry!" Carmen cried as her brother twisted in agony beneath her. She held it to his skin for a long time, and he let out every foul and wretched sound imaginable in his anguish. Finally, she took it off of him and stood up, backing away to the wall.

She held the flashlight on him as Tommy turned over onto his hands and knees, panting. He pressed a hand to his neck. Then he started crying. "Ow," he moaned as tears streamed down his face.

"Tommy?" Carmen asked.

He turned his head and looked up at her, and she saw humanity in his eyes.

"Tommy, are you okay?"

"What happened?" he asked. "Where am I?" He looked down at the piece of metal in his hand and then he tossed it away, confused why he was holding it.

"Oh Tommy," Carmen said, rushing up to him and embracing him. "I'm so sorry. It'll all be okay." She stroked his filthy hair.

Carmen held the flashlight limply in her hand, and it was pointed at the doorway to the last room in the basement. Her eyes widened as she saw a low, creeping fog come out of the room. It was black, like someone poured smoke across the ground. A hat rose up out of it, staying low, and it glided across the floor to them.

"Tommy, watch out!" Carmen shouted as she tried to stand both of them up.

But the witch grabbed hold of his ankle and dragged him into the other room. Tommy's little hands balled up and dragged across the floor as he cried out for his sister, his face a horror show.

Through the doorway to the other room, the floating wraith of the witch rose up into the air and stayed suspended for only a moment before she slammed down through the floor with incredible force and speed, splintering the wood into a thousand pieces, causing a shockwave to rush through the basement. Tommy's body flipped upside down into the air from his ankle and then it whipped around and he was pulled into the hole along with the witch in the blink of an eye. His screams faded.

"Tommy!" Carmen screamed. She rushed up to the edge of the hole, which encapsulated most of the other room, and she shone the flashlight down into the blackness. A long, long tunnel stretched down deep into the earth, and a coldness born from its very depths rose up and touched her. She shivered, her teeth chattering in absolute terror.

Ladder rungs were bolted into the concrete wall of the shaft, and they went as far down as the light could illuminate.

If she wanted to save her brother, she would have to go down.

— CHAPTER TWENTY-FIVE —

DESCENT

The cold depths of the shaft seemed to stretch on forever, burying farther and farther into the earth. Her hands were freezing on the frigid metal rungs. She held the flashlight in her teeth and carefully climbed down. One false move and she would slip off to her death. She tried looking up to see how far she had gone, but vertigo set in, and she clung tightly to the rungs, terrified that she was going to fall.

As she slowly descended, her arm ached where Tommy had slashed her, but she didn't have time to look at the damage. She felt blood trickling down her arm and start to dry as a dull throb coursed through her.

Something appeared in the flashlight below, and as she strained her eyes to see it, she saw that it was solid ground. Her heart leapt in joy, and when she finally reached it, her feet clapped against the cement and echoed all the way up through the shaft. There was a dark tunnel in front of her, but first she pointed the flashlight up to look at where she had come from, and it was so high up that she couldn't see the floor of the basement above her. She turned the light back to the tunnel and crept forward, hearing a distant drip of water in the strange catacombs.

The tunnel gave way to a large, open room, dotted with pillars stretching up to the high ceiling. All the missing children from town were sitting bound with their backs tied to the pillars. Cloth was stuffed in each of their mouths and their wrists were tied behind them with tight ropes.

There had to be at least a hundred children. The ones that could see her, turned their faces with wide eyes and started struggling against their restraints, desperate for her to save them.

Carmen was shocked. They were all alive, but seeing them here like this broke her heart in half. Some of them were dressed down to their underwear and shivering, and all of them were filthy, with dirt caked on their faces and streaked through their hair. Some of them must have been down here for days, and Carmen prayed that none had been killed. She rushed up to the nearest pillar and tried untying the ropes as the children struggled and pleaded under their gags for her help.

"No! Don't!" someone yelled in the distance.

Carmen's head snapped up. "*Tommy!*" she whispered. She looked at the children woefully, but she stood up. If her brother was in imminent danger, she had to help him first. There was another tunnel that stretched off on the other end of the large room, and she trotted quickly through it, trying to stay silent and not make her presence known to the witch.

She heard bubbling liquid in the distance, and she saw a soft orange glow painted on the wall ahead of her as the tunnel went around a corner. She rounded it and the path came into another room, smaller this time. Extended ahead of her was a long row of tables filled with tools, trinkets, and items. There was a set of stairs to her right that led up to a raised area overlooking the rest of the room. A steel railing closed it in, and three large pillars dotted between the railing, stretching up to the ceiling.

Carmen glanced up and saw the edge of the witch's robes from her low angle. It looked like she was bent over something.

"Please, don't!" Tommy said.

Carmen could hear him struggling against his restraints, but she couldn't see him. She moved quickly up the stairs, staying low and peeking over the top of them.

A large black cauldron sat near the far wall in the elevated area, and the witch stewarded over it, plucking a centipede off of a small table next to her and dropping it into the bubbling liquid. A small splash came out of it and an effervescent glow emitted from the brew as it changed to a vibrant magenta color.

Tommy and Brett were both tied up next to the cauldron on the floor. The witch cast glances at the two boys periodically as she dropped ingredients into the brew. Horror was painted on their faces as they watched her, knowing their time would soon come.

The witch grabbed a handful of weeds and scattered them in the liquid, changing it green, and causing an appropriately-colored glow to fill the area.

THE WITCH OF HALLOWEEN HOUSE

Carmen saw that the pillars were wide enough for her to hide behind, and when the witch wasn't looking, she rushed up the edge of the stairs to the first one and concealed herself behind it.

Small tables and items sat between the pillars, and Carmen looked down at a table near her, spotting a strange doll sitting on it. It was like a little ragdoll, and it was dressed in a police officer's uniform. A pin was stuck in the back of its neck.

Carmen silently gasped. She picked it up and looked it over in her hands, knowing that the witch had been using this to control her father. She gingerly clutched the knob of the pin with her fingers, and she slowly pulled it out, placing the pin quietly on the table. She rubbed the back of the doll's neck, then she quietly stuffed it in her coat, hoping that her dad felt better now. She leaned forward and peeked around the column.

The witch scooped up a loose pile of children's clothing with her pale hand and sowed it into the bubbling cauldron. The liquid splashed and jumped, turning to a bright red. She cackled in delight, a strange, terrifying sound, and it reverberated along all the walls in these catacombs. She dipped her hand into the liquid, and Carmen cringed, wondering how hot it must have been. It wouldn't scald the witch, but it certainly would a little boy or girl. The witch pulled up a handful of the red potion to her mouth and drank it. She scooped her hand in again and drank more, soon greedily lapping it up and making horrifying noises.

Carmen watched in disgust, leaning around the pillar just enough to see, as she put a hand to her mouth. She glanced over at Tommy and saw that he was staring at the witch in amazement and horror, then her eyes fell on Brett. Brett was staring back at her. Carmen tried to put a finger to her lips to tell him to be quiet, but it was too late.

"Help!" Brett screamed at her. "Help us!"

The witch's head snapped up and turned in her direction immediately.

Carmen's blood ran cold as she backed away from the pillar, reaching her hand into her coat for the iron knife.

The witch shrieked, and the earsplitting sound bounced around the walls ceaselessly.

Carmen pressed her hands to her ears in pain.

The witch hunched forward suddenly, and the glowing, translucent skin of her hands and face seemed to move across her body, like it was swapping places, and then the flesh turned opaque, settling on a solid pale yellow. The sound of something ripping filled the room, and the witch's body convulsed. Her robes were shredded in the back where long legs like spiders grew out, stretching out and finally growing down to the floor. The bones in her fingers solidified and turned into sharp talons. The white hair grew long out of her head, falling down to the floor and sweeping across it, and her face twisted, growing hard, bulging ridges in her forehead as her teeth sharpened into razors. Her body grew to twice her normal size, and then her mutations finally stopped. She turned her attention back on Carmen, now a freakish hybrid between human and beast, like this was a transition from ethereal wisp back to full humanity.

She bent forward and placed her hands on the floor, clicking her talons against the cement as her head snapped up and locked on to Carmen. The long legs coming out of her back fidgeted and oriented her to face her prey.

And then the horrifying creature came for her, her legs moving at a blistering speed along the ground.

— CHAPTER TWENTY-SIX —

WITCH'S BREW

"Carmen, get out of here!" Tommy shouted.

She turned and ran down the stairs, fleeing for the tunnel as the witch chased her. She whipped the flashlight over her shoulder and saw the witch entering the tunnel behind her. Her legs and talons clicked across the floor, then she seamlessly moved onto the wall as she ran, then the ceiling above her.

Carmen yelped as she rounded the corner and ran as fast as she could into the open area where the children were bound. She turned around when she got to the big room and backed up, watching the witch climb out of the tunnel and up the wall. She pointed the flashlight up and followed her, but the ceiling was so high that she couldn't see it, and the witch disappeared into the shadows.

Carmen backed up, her mouth hanging open, as she listened. Behind the struggling cries of the children, she could hear the soft clicking of the witch's legs from far away. Dust occasionally sifted down from above, and Carmen kept away from it. She stretched the flashlight up a pillar, slowly walking around it from where the dust had come down, trying to catch sight.

She didn't even notice as the witch slowly and silently crept down a pillar behind her.

A jet of red shot over Carmen's shoulder, missing her by an inch, and she dove forward and fell to the ground. Twisting over onto her back, she looked and saw the witch extending her wand in one of her taloned hands. The beam of magic shot between the pillars and hit the far wall of the room, causing a chunk of concrete to burst apart and rain down on the children nearby as they shielded their heads.

Carmen got up to her feet and ran away from the witch as the creature cast more spells at her. She fumbled for the witch mirror hanging around her neck, and when she suddenly found herself backed into a corner with the witch closing in behind her, she spun around and held it up.

The witch cast another red bolt at her, and it bounced off of the rose-colored stone, which was glowing intensely now, and reflected back at the witch. The bolt struck her in the shoulder and knocked her over onto her back as she shrieked and smoke came out of the spot where it hit her. The witch used her spiderlike legs to right herself, then she retreated up a pillar, climbing over the terrified children and disappearing into the darkness looming up at the ceiling.

Carmen moved the flashlight around, but she didn't hear or see anything. She swept it across the room, looking at the children, then she noticed a body lying between some pillars in the middle of the room.

It was Stacy.

Carmen rushed over to her and rolled her onto her back. "Stacy..." She gently patted her cheek. "Stacy!"

Stacy's eyes slowly fluttered open and she groaned. The boils that had covered her whole face and hands had receded, but a few red marks remained. She slowly sat up, and looked around, not knowing where she was. "What's going on?" she asked.

Carmen tried to help her up, but Stacy batted her away, getting up to her feet on her own.

"Don't touch me!" she cried, holding her hands up in the air in disgust. "I'm finding Brett and then getting out of here," she said, then she turned and walked toward the tunnel leading to the tall shaft.

"Stacy, wait..." Carmen saved the rest of her breath, realizing it was worthless.

As Stacy came to the opening of the tunnel, the witch dropped from the ceiling and slammed onto the floor behind her. Stacy turned around and screamed as she saw the horrid creature. Then the witch charged, lifting one of its legs in the air, ready to stab it through her.

"Don't!" Carmen cried as she jumped and tackled Stacy out of the way. The sharp end of the witch's leg cut through the top of Carmen's shoulder, giving her a nasty gash and making her spin like a top on the floor. She hit the cement hard and grunted, whimpering from the pain.

Stacy got up to her knees and looked at Carmen in disbelief. A moment ago, she was sure she would be dead, but Carmen had saved her life. She never in a million years would have imagined that Carmen would do something like that for her. "You... You saved my..." Then she fell quiet, because she simply didn't have the words.

Carmen weakly pushed herself up to her hands and knees as the witch made a circle around a few of the columns, and then she came around for them again. "Our brothers are tied up down that tunnel," Carmen said, pointing and wincing from the pain in her shoulder. "You have to free them."

Stacy was still speechless from Carmen's heroic act, but she got up to her feet and quickly made her way for the tunnel, glancing over her shoulder for the witch.

But the witch set her sights back on Carmen. She lined herself up down the aisle of pillars and came for her, keeping her spells to herself now that she knew Carmen had the witch mirror, and instead just physically attacked her.

Carmen ducked as another leg swept by, trying to take her head off, and it burst through the edge of a pillar, knocking concrete everywhere. The children screamed below and shielded themselves as a dusty rain fell on them.

The witch swiveled around again, and Carmen took off, trying to tie up the witch and keep some pillars and distance between them. It was a cat and mouse game that played out repeatedly as she tried to hold the witch at bay, but she was fast and agile, despite her size.

"Carmen!" Tommy cried from the mouth of the tunnel.

She pointed the flashlight at him and saw him standing there in his now-filthy red sweater. Brett and Stacy were behind him, and they all watched in horror as the witch cast another spell at her, this time her green ensnarement spell, while she wasn't looking. The green cord wrapped around her ankle, and she fell on the floor. She spun over on her back and watched in horror as the witch dragged her closer, holding up her arms and twirling her talons through the air as she gnashed her teeth.

Carmen looked around, not knowing what to do. She reached inside her coat and pulled out the dagger that she'd wrapped up in cloth at the church. Frantically unbundling it, she held it and tried cutting the cord with it.

And it worked; the green cord snapped immediately and flung back at the witch like it was made of elastic. The witch shrieked in displeasure and charged at her again. But Carmen got up to her feet and backed up, holding the knife out in front of her.

The witch skidded to a stop, understanding what she was holding and not wanting to charge into it. They came to a standstill, and they slowly circled around each other, one of them occasionally putting a pillar between them and coming out the other side still staring at each other.

Carmen glanced over at Tommy who was still standing dumbfounded at the edge of the room, and she called his name. He perked up and watched her reach into her coat, surreptitiously pulling out the box of salt and the bag full of garlic bulbs that she'd brought. She kept these hidden from the witch as she backed up, pulling their duel toward Tommy. She circled around as the witch watched, putting a pillar between them, and Carmen quickly bent down when she was out of view. She set down the items behind it, then she stood up again and walked out from the pillar as if she hadn't done anything. Then, in an act of incredible bravery that she didn't know she possessed, she ran at the witch, thrusting the knife at her. The witch backed up and swung two of her legs in a scissor motion at her head.

Carmen ducked and rolled on the ground, then she dove for a pillar as the witch cast another spell. She got up and ran to the opposite end of the room as Tommy snuck in and grabbed the items, knowing exactly what to do with them. With Carmen drawing the witch away toward the other corner, Stacy and Brett ran into the room, hurrying to untie the nearest children to them, who were all sobbing in sheer terror.

Tommy ran through the tunnel, climbing up the stairs as quickly as he could for the cauldron. He saw the red glow dancing on the wall as the liquid bubbled. But then he tripped over the last stair, falling forward and dropping the items on the ground. The box of salt hit the cement and split open, spilling out onto the floor. "Crap!" he said, pulling the box upright. He stuff the broken box and bag of garlic under his arm, then he tried to scoop up as much spilled salt as he could. He waddled over to the cauldron and dumped his handful of salt in. He poured the rest of the salt from the box, and then he ripped the bag open and watched as the garlic bulbs tumbled out and splashed in the red murk.

The liquid bubbled and flashed, and its color turned a little darker, but still stayed red. Tommy gulped, hoping the witch wouldn't notice.

Out in the large room, Carmen stood at one end of it, shining the flashlight down a row of half-broken pillars. The witch stood at the other end, and the two of them stared each other down. Then the witch charged. She carried the front two of her legs in the air as she came for Carmen, and she held her arms out too, reaching out her clawed talons for her and gnashing her teeth as her eyes swam crazily in her head and she shrieked an unintelligible string of words.

Carmen stood her ground, ready to duck behind a pillar, like she was a matador with a bull. But as soon as she wanted to move, her shoe slipped on a layer of dust on the floor, and her legs came out from under her. She hit the cement, and knocked her chin against it, disorienting her.

The witch closed in, and before she could get away, one of the witch's legs came down and stabbed her in the thigh.

Carmen screamed and squirmed around on her back in pain. She looked down at the large, sharp end of the leg digging into her, and she gazed up at the witch as she closed in on her, ready to devour her. Her mind was running at a frenzied pace, and in her desperation, knowing she was about to die, all she could think to do was to slash the knife at the witch's leg.

The blade of the knife cut through it like it was butter, and the witch immediately retracted it and shrieked with such force that the walls shook. Carmen covered her ears, and the witch held her injured leg up in the air and stared at it in horror. Then she turned and fled for the tunnel leading to her cauldron, keeping it off the ground.

Tommy was just coming around the corner in the tunnel, and he had to dive toward the wall to avoid her.

"Carmen, are you okay?!" Stacy asked, rushing over to her aid. Both she and Brett helped her up, and she limped over to the tunnel where the witch had gone.

Tommy watched from the edge of the room as the witch's legs clicked up the stairs for the cauldron. When she got there, she immediately plunged her injury into the liquid. Her body bent low over it, using her taloned hands to scoop up some more potion into her mouth, feeling relieved now that she had her elixir.

Then the witch's eyes went wide. She yanked her mutated leg out of the cauldron as if it were lava, then she scuttled backward like a bug. She shrieked again and all the tables and implements on them rattled and tipped over.

Carmen, Stacy and Brett came into the room, and Tommy looked over his shoulder at them, then he pointed out the witch.

"I think it worked," he said.

The witch spun around and held a gnarled hand to her chest. She looked at the four of them in shock, like she had just experienced the ultimate betrayal. She began coughing and sputtering, and her legs weakened. Her whole abomination of a body stumbled around the upper area of the room like she was drunk. She retched, trying to spit out the potion she drank, but it was too late. Her body started to wither, like a dead bug being baked in the sun. In desperation, she stumbled back to the cauldron, trying to take another drink of it, but then she spit it out and backed away from it, unable to stop the terrible disease coursing through her.

"Help me up there," Carmen said to the others, and they ran to her sides and brought her up the stairs.

The witch's back was turned, still in the throes of madness and desperation as her body continued to shrink and wither. Her once-thick legs had now shriveled up into thin and brittle sticks, and the skin on her body drooped severely. She spun around suddenly and was met with the blade of the iron knife.

Carmen plunged it deep into her heart.

The witch looked down with a look of horror. Then the look slowly faded as she lost the strength to do even that. The effects of the metal compounded what the potion had done to her, and she shrieked one last time, this time very weakly. Her whole body collapsed in on itself, and she pulled herself off the knife, stumbling back into the cauldron. She tripped over it and fell headfirst into the bubbling liquid as her body shrunk into nothing before their very eyes.

The liquid splashed and black smoke came out of the concoction. It rumbled and splattered violently for a time, turning the liquid jet-black, then the smoke receded and the four of them watched as the liquid bubbled down to nothing, leaving a thin black film of viscous sludge on the inside of the cauldron.

Carmen let out a sigh of relief, and she stumbled backward, feeling weak as the others caught her.

A little laugh escaped Tommy's lips.

They looked at him.

"What's so funny?" Carmen asked.

He looked at his sister, smiling. "We did it."

— CHAPTER TWENTY-SEVEN —

THE SPELL SHATTERED

Carmen finally reached the top of the long ladder, and she carefully climbed up onto the broken floor in the basement of the house. She moved through the doorway to the other room and watched as Brett and Stacy came up behind her, followed by Randy and Shawn and some of the older children. Tommy had elected to stay down with the rest of them, untying them and comforting them until help arrived.

The group got up the ladder safely, and then they all went up the stairs and left Halloween House once and for all.

They were greeted by the cold light of the November morning, and things immediately seemed more peaceful than they had been in the last few days. The birds chirped busily in the trees, and little critters scampered through the woods, looking for nuts. The kids stretched themselves out, working out the kinks and pains of their injuries, and they scanned the woods around them.

A group of people moved through the trees down below. When one person in the group spotted them, they turned and called out for the others. Soon a whole mob of townspeople gathered around the house, and Robert stepped out in front of them, his eyes falling on his daughter. "Where's Tommy?"

"He's in the house," Carmen said quickly. "Don't worry, he's fine."

Once his greatest fear was assuaged, a smile—a genuine smile—came over Robert's face.

He didn't say a word. He just walked in and hugged Carmen. She didn't even care about the pain in her shoulder. She hugged him back, tightly.

He held his daughter at arm's length, looking down at the nasty gashes in her shoulder and leg, as well as the slashed arm of her coat. "Are you okay?"

"Yeah," she said. "A little banged up."

"But you're alive."

They smiled at each other and hugged again, and tears streamed out of Carmen's face now that she had her father back again.

"Tommy's down there with all the other kids," Carmen said. "They're alive."

A wave of relief rushed through the crowd, and many of them broke into tears, being the very parents of the missing children. Now that the spell had broken on all of them, they had remembered all of their actions vividly, and were struggling to come to terms with some of the things they had done.

"How many?" Robert asked.

"I don't know," Carmen said, "a hundred, maybe. All of them."

Robert looked over at the house. "How on earth can that house fit a hundred in the basement?"

"No, I mean *down*, down there," she said, bending over and holding her hand just above her feet.

Robert's eyes widened. "Oh."

— — —

It only took a few hours for the townspeople to get some equipment in the basement and bring the kids up safely on a pulley system. When the last of them was out, Tommy rode up in the little elevator and was pulled out of the shaft.

Robert hugged him tightly and tears came out of his eyes, glad that his son was okay, and Tommy was glad that he had his dad back.

"What are you going to do with this place?" he asked his father.

Robert peered down the dark hole and brushed his fingers across his mustache. "I don't know. I guess we'll seal it off. Treat it like an old mineshaft and bulldoze the house."

When they all left the basement and walked outside the house, Robert turned around and stood next to Don, and the two of them stared wistfully at the blackened remains of what the kids always called Halloween House. They thought back to just before that Halloween when the two of them came up alone and served the search warrant on the woman. It all seemed so long ago, and such a crazy incident when looked at through the filter of recent events.

"Can you believe it?" Robert said to Don. "A single missing boy started this whole chain of events..."

Don nodded. "Yeah, crazy, isn't it?"

"Or maybe more like a single fire," Robert said. "A whole town went crazy on its own, without any spells or magic. All it took was a spark."

"A single, vengeful idiot, you mean," Don said.

Brett stood by, feeling embarrassed. "It was only a prank," he muttered.

Robert was about to muse how they still never found out who set the fire, then his eyes sharpened on Brett. "What did you say, son?"

Brett realized his mistake, and he looked at Robert in horror.

"What did you just say?" he asked again. "Did you start that fire?"

"I... um..."

Tommy stepped forward. "I started the fire, Dad," he said. "I never told you because I knew you'd be mad."

His father looked at him.

"It was just supposed to be a prank. I told Brett about it after, and I made him promise not to tell anyone else."

"Explain yourself, boy," Robert said sternly, anger arching his eyebrows.

Tommy stuttered, looking for the words. "I... I saw everyone standing around, and I thought it would be funny to light a fire behind the house and make the witch come out. But she never did. I'm really sorry, I didn't mean to."

Brett stared at Tommy in shock.

Robert looked down at his son with intense disappointment. "We'll talk about this later," he said. "For now, we've got to get home and recuperate."

As the crowd started to disperse down the hill, Brett walked over to Tommy and nudged him. Tommy turned to him.

"Why did you do that?" Brett asked.

Tommy shrugged. "I knew it made you feel bad, and I didn't want you to feel bad."

Brett nodded slowly, struggling to understand his reasoning. But he was thankful that Tommy did that. As he looked at Tommy, a strange, almost alien feeling rose up in him. "Thank you," he said.

Robert, Carmen and Tommy stood in the woods, watching everyone else leave with their children. He notified the state level, and they were on their way with some help to rebuild, but for now he needed to get his children to safety. He turned and looked at his daughter.

She saw him staring at her injuries, and she said, "It's okay, Dad. I can walk. I'm just going to be a little slow."

"Nonsense," he said, then he bent and swept her off her feet, holding her in his arms.

She giggled, feeling like Daddy's little girl again for the first time since her mother died.

Robert crouched down and grabbed Tommy's hand, and the three of them made their way back to town.

"I know you didn't start that fire," Robert said to Tommy.

Tommy looked up at him. "How did you know?" he asked, dumbfounded.

Robert smiled. "A good police chief always knows. But that was very brave of you to cover for a friend like that."

Tommy nodded slowly, staring out into the distance and appreciating the wisdom.

— — —

Carmen lay in her hospital bed, fiddling with the edge of her gown. She stared at the clock on the wall and watched the time tick away. She sighed.

Her father and brother had just stopped in to visit her along with a couple of her friends from college. Even Peter stopped by with her father's permission, apologizing for being incapacitated and not able to help her defeat the witch. Carmen apologized for her father, and her father also apologized to Peter for mistreatment. All around, everyone in the town had a heavy cloud of regret hanging over them.

The doctors performed some surgery on Carmen's injuries, and they said she would make a speedy recovery, but she didn't agree with their definition of "speedy" anymore. She picked up the remote off the bedside table and turned on the TV, mindlessly flipping channels. But it was all just noise to her, and she shut it off. Her head sank down against the pillow and she let out a long breath.

There was a knock at her door.

Carmen looked over and saw Stacy peeking in. "Oh, Stacy... What are you doing here?"

"I just came to visit," Stacy said. "Can I come in?"

"Yeah, of course. Sorry..."

Carmen pushed herself up in her bed as Stacy opened the door and walked in the room, holding a bouquet of flowers.

"Oh, you didn't have to do that," Carmen said, smiling.

"I think I did," Stacy replied, setting them down on the table next to her. "Just to apologize for being... well, a bitch. And for saving my life."

Carmen played it off. "Ah, it was no big deal."

Stacy smirked. "What, you do that every Halloween?"

"Every other Halloween," Carmen said, smirking back.

Stacy sat down on the edge of the bed and stared at the wall in front of her. "I've been so terrible to everyone all these years," she said. "So stuck inside my own head, caring what everyone else thinks. But you're different. You always do the right thing. You just... you're a good person, Carmen."

Carmen blushed. "Well, sometimes you just gotta grab life by the—"

Vince poked his head in the room. "There you are, Baby," he said. "I was looking all over the place for you."

He barged right in without paying any attention to Carmen. "Come on, let's go."

"Vince, what are you doing here?" Stacy asked, anger on her face.

"What does it looked like, Baby? I'm coming to pick you up. I heard you were here visiting someone." He glanced at Carmen at last but didn't even give her a nod. He looked over at the flowers. "You didn't buy these, did you, Baby? I told you not to spend money on stupid things like this!"

"Vince, get out of here!" Stacy said. "I told you, we're through."

"We ain't through," he said. He walked up to her with a fiery look in his eyes, as if asking her how dare she say something like that to him. He sank down on the bed, landing on Carmen's bad leg, and she bolted upright in bed with tears in her eyes. Vince adjusted himself off of it, but he didn't pay any attention to her. "You're coming with me... *now*." He grabbed her by the wrist.

Stacy grabbed him by the crotch.

Vince's eyes went as wide as dinner plates.

She stood up and pulled him off the bed, squeezing harder. She heard a little whimper escape his throat, and she dragged him back toward the door and slammed him against the wall, never letting go of her grip. She was tired of being pushed around by jerks, and letting them walk all over her and Brett. They were nothing but a bad influence, and now that part of her was over forever. She got right in his face as tears came out of his eyes.

"Do you need your ears cleaned out?" Stacy asked. "You and I are through. For good. If you ever come near me again... if you ever come near Brett again... I won't be so nice next time. Understand?"

He nodded rapidly, his face twisting in pain.

"Now get... *out* of here!" She shoved him through the open doorway, and he crashed into a gurney, tipping it over as he fell to the ground. The orderlies in the hall stared at him, and Vince pushed himself up to his feet, his face reddening. Embarrassed, he pulled his jacket straight, then he headed for the nearest stairwell.

Carmen smiled at Stacy as she turned around. "Well look at you, grabbing life by the balls."

― ― ―

Carmen and Tommy sat at the dinner table, and Robert waltzed into the room carrying a large platter. "Dinner is served!" he said, laying it on the table.

Carmen was a few weeks out of the hospital, and feeling much better, though the doctors told her to be careful for a while on her leg and her shoulder. She put a hand on her father's arm and smiled at him. "I'm really glad you're spending more time with us, Dad," she said.

"I wouldn't miss it for the world, Sweetpea," he said, looking at Tommy and rustling his hair. "From now on, I'm going to be shifting around the officers' hours, and giving myself a little more time off."

Tommy couldn't have been happier to hear him say that as he fixed his hair.

The kids started pulling dinner from the platter onto their plates, but before they dug in, Robert stopped them.

He stared down at his wedding band on his finger, and fiddled with it. "Why don't we say a little prayer before dinner tonight?" he suggested.

Tommy gave him a strange look. "But Dad, we're not religious."

"Not really a prayer, then," Robert said. "But I think it would be nice to remember your mom... maybe say a few memories you have of her."

Carmen smiled, happy that he was including her in this. For the first time in years, it felt like their happy family was complete again.

The three of them went around, sharing some happy memories, and they all laughed and smiled as they remembered the matron saint who was the glue in their family. When they finished, they all resolved to always keep her in their memories with everything they did. They ate their dinner in peace and quiet, a constant smile on each of their faces.

"So does that mean you'll take me to the arcade sometime?" Tommy asked halfway through dinner.

Robert smiled. "I'll tell you what, I'll even take you trick-or-treating next year."

"You will?" Tommy asked with excitement.

"Of course. I'll even take the whole day off work if I have to. Just you and me, what do you say?"

Carmen was thrilled beyond belief to see her little brother smile again like this. The whole town quickly went back to normal as everyone healed from their terrible ordeal. They had still lost a few of them in senseless accidents or tragedies under the witch's spell, but as the years went on, they forgot that that terrible house on the hill—and the witch inside of it—ever even existed.

Thank you so much for reading! If you enjoyed this book, please consider leaving an honest review on Amazon. It really helps me get more eyes on my books, and in turn allows me to write more books for my fans!

Visit my website for FREE stories and news of future releases, promotions, and sales:
www.jeffdegordick.com

Say hello on my Facebook and Twitter page:
www.facebook.com/jeffdegordickauthor
www.twitter.com/jeffdegordick

I'm happy to hear from my readers! Send me an email at:
jeff@jeffdegordick.com

Also by Jeff DeGordick:
The Haunting of Bloodmoon House
The Haunting of Jingle House

ABOUT THE AUTHOR

Jeff DeGordick is a horror novelist currently living in southern Ontario, Canada. Writing stories was his first passion as a child, but he's also had forays into testing and designing video games for a living, and a very brief career as a cook.

He began writing in 1994 at age seven, embarking on a long journey of spinning strange and scary tales, penning many short stories and partial novels as a hobby.

He is also the author of the Zombie Apocalypse Series and he's currently writing many more creepy tales!

Printed in Great Britain
by Amazon